The Real World Series
and
Another Year in the Bronx

Two Stories by Andrew Laz

PublishAmerica
Baltimore

First printing

ISBN: 1-60703-199-X (softcover)
ISBN:978-1-4489-1617-7 (hardcover)
PUBLISHED BY PUBLISHAMERICA, LLLP
www.publishamerica.com
Baltimore

Printed in the United States of America

The Real World Series

Chapter 1

It started innocently enough. After the 2006 season, Major League Baseball sponsored a tournament designed to promote the game around the world. The premise was simple, an elimination tournament. Anyone could enter, but professionals would not be allowed to play. After the elimination rounds, the winner would play a three game series with a Major League all-star team, a fantasy series complete with photo ops and autograph signings. Different stars were signed to make it a special event. The commissioner's office hoped that the tournament would develop millions of new fans around the world.

Since professionals were barred, and since some of the entries were from areas like Cambodia and Somalia where baseball wasn't played, the early rounds of the tournament were expected to resemble slow pitch softball games. No one was surprised when final scores were 33 to 28 with upwards of thirty walks a game. The umpires were instructed to call a generous strike zone to keep the games moving. The good will from the round robin games was exactly what baseball had projected. Alex Rodriguez, Derek Jeter and Jason Giambi from the New York Yankees traveled to Kuala Lumpur to participate in opening round ceremonies and give batting tips to eager youngsters. Other Major Leaguers went to Africa and Eastern Europe with similar missions. At the beginning, all seemed to be going exactly according to plan.

Unnoticed by the tournament commissioners, a strange set of events was unfolding in the regional taking place in Nepal, where teams from Tibet, East Timor, Islamabad and Sri Lanka were competing to advance. The team from East Timor, a location that most of the rest of the world had never even heard of, was winning their games by the mercy rule, 35 to 0, after the second inning. The tournament sponsors, not wanting to embarrass any team in a "Good Will" tournament, had created a mercy rule as follows: A regular nine inning game would be declared a victory if either team was ahead by ten runs after eight innings, 15 after 7, 20 after 6, 25 after 5, 30 after 4, or 35 after 3 or 2.

No one paid much attention as the scores were reported to the league office in New York. The common assumption was that there must have been a couple of college players that settled in East Timor, and that the rest of the teams in their pool must have been brand new to the game.

As the tournament progressed, Major League Baseball was busy planning festivities for the gala final series celebration. Players were signed up to make appearances and play a few innings. Rooms were booked for dances and parties. Celebrities were scheduled to attend. The commissioner paid little attention to the games in the preliminary rounds. Instead, he was busy contacting old timers like 72-year-old Willie Mays and 70-year-old Sandy Koufax. Hopefully they would play in game two of the championship series thus creating media interest while guaranteeing the amateur team one victory to set up a 'dramatic' final game.

The best teams were expected to come from North America, Latin America, Korea and Japan. However, strange things started happening. After the preliminary rounds and super regionals, the teams with the best records advancing to the semifinals were Korea, The Dominican

Republic, Japan and East Timor. No one gave it much thought that East Timor had advanced. After all, they had achieved their record beating up on teams like Ghana and Luxembourg. Most of the Major League teams sent scouts to the semifinals to look at the talented young college players from Japan, many of whom would be big league prospects. Sadaharu Oh, the great Japanese slugger was managing his country's team. At a press conference the day before the finals started, he was asked about his team's chances. In his normal humble manner, he praised the Dominican and Korean teams. "They have some very talented players," he commented. "Our boys will have to play our best baseball to beat them."

"What about East Timor?" one of the reporters asked.

The great Oh chuckled. "I am sure that they will be formidable opposition," he answered.

The tournament resumed the next afternoon. Major league scouts and 50,000 other fans crowded Giants stadium in Tokyo where they watched Japan beat the Dominican Republic three to two in a Major League quality game. The game was a duel between two pitchers with ninety-five mile per hour fastballs, sliders that broke late and great command of the strike zone. Predictably, the game was played without errors, and the small ball, bunts, sacrifices, base running, etc. was executed perfectly. Because the game went thirteen innings, it was eleven o'clock at night before the next game started. All but a handful of the crowd went home to be rested for Japan's championship game against Korea assuming they would eliminate East Timor in the second half of the double header. The Japanese press promoted the game as a grudge match, playing off the political tensions of centuries-old conflict between Japan and Korea, hatred that had been fueled by the recent aggressiveness of North Korea's nuclear program. Not surprisingly, there had been accusations in the Japanese press that Korea was using professionals playing under aliases, possibly some of the players from the team that had beaten the United States in the World Baseball Classic.

Imagine the surprise of the Japanese team and the rest of the world when they woke up the next morning to find out that they would be playing East Timor instead of Korea. East Timor had trounced the Korea team in the second game by a score of thirty-five to nothing after two innings.

The Japanese press was stunned. Back in the United States in the commissioner's office, summer interns were busy putting together press kits for the Japan-Korea game when they heard the news. Bud Selig called his assistant on site in Tokyo. When assured that the press report was accurate, and that East Timor had demolished the mighty Korea, his only comment was, "Who the fuck are those guys? Don't they know that letting them in the tournament was just a joke to begin with?"

Needless to say, as the word got out that about East Timor's victory, moods changed. Owners and general managers of every Major League team cancelled their plans and headed to the airports. New York Yankee Number One, nicknamed The Yankee Clipper, was rolled out of its hanger at JFK. There, an unshaven Brian Cashman met Joe Torre. The two baseball executives boarded the jet heading non-stop for Tokyo.

Chapter 2

The next day, a standing room only crowd jammed into the Tokyo Dome, curious to get a glimpse of East Timor. There were no articles in the newspapers about the Korean massacre the night before as none of the reporters had stayed to watch the game. The defeated Koreans had left immediately without giving any interviews. Fans lined up outside the gates to observe the East Timor players when they arrived at the stadium and ask for autographs. They were in their seats early to watch East Timor's batting practice. Much to everyone's disappointment, none of the players took the field at their assigned practice time. In the press box, officials were frantically trying to find anyone who spoke the East Timorean language to help with player announcements and possibly do some interviews. Finally, they were able to locate Roa Amolin, an East Timorean national, a visiting professional at Kyodo University.

When Roa came up to the booth, Vince Scully on loan from Major League Baseball to broadcast the final game, asked about the baseball program in East Timor. "You must have an impressive organization to field this kind of team. Tell us about your program."

"We no play baseball," Roa replied in broken English.

"Tell us about your practice facilities."

"There are no baseball fields in East Timor," Roa answered.

So much for the pregame interview.

Television stations expecting to provide local coverage of batting practice and other pregame activities scrambled to replace special features they had prepared for the Japan-Korea contest as their cameras stared at the empty field. After what seemed an eternity, it was finally game time.

East Timor was designated the visiting team. They would bat first. In the booth, Scully was handed the lineup card. "There must be some mistake," he thought to himself. "All of the players in the lineup have the same name." There it was in black and white, batting first Snemelc A. Regor, batting second Snemelc B. Regor, batting third Snemelc C. Regor, and so forth with Snemelc I. Regor batting ninth. The lineup card reminded Scully of a second-rate movie in which as a joke all of the Greek characters were named Costas. Not knowing what else to do and not wanting to insult any East Timoreans that might be listening, he went ahead and announced the lineup. He was going to announce the bench players too, only to find out that there were only twelve players on the team. Even stranger, there were no coaches or managers on the bench, not even a trainer.

The starting pitcher for Japan, Sudo Niramatsu took his warm-up tosses, and the game was ready to start. Niramatsu was the ace of the Japanese staff. Six foot four, two hundred and thirty pounds, Sudo had been saved for the final game expecting to face Korea. Most of the pro scouts in Japan and America believed that he was the best twenty-year-old pitcher in the world. Blessed with a ninety-eight mile per hour fastball, a wicked slider and a devastating curve, many hailed him as the next Bob Gibson.

Snemelc A. came walking up to the plate. He was tall and thin with big, thick glasses and buckteeth. Long, shaggy hair came down to his collar. As he set himself in the batters box, he seemed to be squinting. Scully didn't say it on the air, but he was the homeliest creature that he had ever seen. Snemelc A. watched the first pitch come in low and away for ball one. "A ninety-six mile an hour fastball," Scully announced. "He probably hasn't seen many of those in East Timor." The next pitch was a fastball down the middle of the plate for strike one. "Looks like he is measuring it," Scully said slightly sarcastically. The third pitch never got to the catcher's mitt. Snemelc turned on it with an easy, effortless swing, and the ball floated into the left field stands. "Boy, did he make that look easy," was all that the announcer could say.

The hometown fans seemed stunned. That was only the second homer that Sudo had given up the whole season. No one could have guessed what happened next. Snemelc B. approached the plate, and as Scully said, "he looked exactly like Snemelc A." The first pitch was a changeup. Snemelc took an easy swing, another home run. The score was two to nothing.

One after another, the seemingly identical batters hit long, lazy fly ball homers. Fastballs, curves, sliders, high, low, inside or outside, it didn't matter, the East Timoreans launched homers all landing in almost the identical spot in the left field stands. The team batted around without an out until they reached twenty runs, the maximum allowed under the mercy rule.

Another oddity was each of the batter's mannerisms. As soon as they stepped in the batters box, they shed their geeky personas and acted just like Major Leaguers. Some smoothed out the dirt. Others tapped their bat on the plate. They spit. They scratched their groins. They adjusted their batting gloves. None of it made any sense, but they laid it on thick, almost as if they were priming for style points.

In the bottom of the inning, the East Timor team took the field in an unorthodox manner. None of the fielders took any grounders or practicc throws to loosen up their arms. Snemelc I. didn't use any of his nine warm up pitches, but as soon as Tora Suzuki stepped up to the plate, he was all business. He smoothed out the dirt in front of the rubber. He tossed the rosin bag. He peered in for signs. Then, he proceeded to strike out Tora on three pitches. "Talk about movement on his fastball!" Vince Scully exclaimed. "Those pitches are just about unhittable."

Regor would have struck out the side with nine pitches, but the umpire called a ball on the third pitch to the next batter. The ball was close to perfect on the outside part of the plate, just a little bit high. Regor peered in at the umpire, put his glove over his mouth as if to mask what he was saying and then proceeded to retire the side.

The next inning was the same as the first. The new Japanese pitcher tried to knock down Snemelc C. on the first pitch, but the batter drew his head back without much effort. Home run followed home run until twenty more runs were on the board. The only suspense was that each batter had their own unique home run trot, each one mimicking former Major Leaguers. The capacity crowd was stunned. Some threw beer and hot dogs onto the field, but most just got up and left. By the bottom half of the inning, the only ones left in the stands were reporters and scouts.

In the bottom of the second with two outs, the home team got a fluke hit. Sachuku Katsui tried to get out of the way of an inside pitch. The ball hit his bat and went dribbling down the line. The third baseman charged and made a great throw but the speedy Katsui was safe on a questionable call. Then, all hell broke loose. One of the spare players came charging out of the East Timor dugout and started arguing with the first base ump. Looking like Earl Weaver, he turned his cap and got into the umpire's face. He shouted and screamed until he was finally ejected.

"Pretty strange for a forty to nothing score," was Scully's comment. Before he left the field, Snemelc L. kicked some dirt, pulled the first base bag out of the ground and knocked over the water cooler. His last act was to throw a bundle of bats out onto the field before he headed to the clubhouse.

"I wonder what happens when he gets really mad?" Scully thought to himself.

In any case, the last batter was retired, and the game was over by the mercy rule after two innings. East Timor would be heading to New York for a three game series to crown the World Baseball Champion.

In the stands, Brian Cashman and Joe Torre were talking to George Steinbrenner on their cell phone. Back in New York, Commissioner Bud Selig, who had been watching the game on satellite, picked up his phone. He wasn't smiling.

Meanwhile, as the last remaining fans filed out of the Tokyo Dome, everyone in attendance was stunned by what they had seen, everyone that is except for two lonely people sitting in the nosebleed seats past the right field foul pole. Binoculars around their neck, they guzzled beer and munched Cracker Jack as they made notes on their laptops. They were both wearing polka dot shirts with pocket protectors and lime green pants. On their red hats were the large letters, MIT.

CHAPTER 3

A Strange Alliance

Twenty-five years earlier, roommates Steve Glickman and Garden Bostwick III graduated from MIT, The Massachusetts Institute of Technology. Glickman had grown up in Roslyn, New York. Steve was tall and thin with red hair and thick glasses. He had never been much of an athlete. In fact, he had struck out three times in a row in a Little League game. At MIT, he studied business administration, but like all boys that grew up in Roslyn, his lifelong ambition was to play or work for the New York Yankees. In Roslyn, no one played basketball or soccer. No one ever talked about football or track. Baseball was the only game in town. Kids listened to every Yankee game. Afterwards, they talked to pals on the phone dissecting every play. For day games, friends would gather at a common house. They would hold their fingers in their ears or under their chins every time Mantle or Maris batted. Maybe the superstition would help the sluggers hit home runs. They wouldn't take a chance that it might not work. At night, when mothers and fathers thought their kids were asleep, they would be listening to the games on earphones connected to their transistor radios. The rite of passage in Roslyn was not making out with your first girl, it was taking the subway through the rough New York neighborhoods to Yankee Stadium for the first time without your parents.

When it became obvious that he would not become the next Hall of Fame shortstop, Steve Glickman set his sights on the Yankees front office. After graduation, with his MIT diploma in hand, Steve turned down multiple, big dollar offers from major corporations to intern for free in the Yankee organization. At first, he was given menial jobs, running contracts to downtown attorneys, booking plane tickets for visiting family, etc. He didn't mind paying his dues. He knew that it was just a matter of time before he would be jetting to LA to make big deals and negotiating contracts with the superstars. After a couple of months, Gene Michael, the General Manager started to ask his opinion on trades and roster moves. Glickman, who had never missed a Yankee game in his whole life (he snuck a radio into his Bar Mitzvah) was perceptive in evaluating the talent. In fact, several of the big trades that Michael put together were actually the product of Steve's mental database. One afternoon, at the end of his internship, he was summoned to report to George Steinbrenner's office. Knowing that this might be the big moment, he ran home over his lunch hour to put on his best suit. As he waited outside the Boss' office looking at the photos of Yankee legends, Steve was filled with excitement. He went through every employment scenario in his mind. The meeting started half an hour late. Steve didn't care. When he was finally called into the office, he fully expected to be praised for his performance and offered a permanent position in the front office. As he walked in, Steinbrenner and Gene Michael were sitting on a couch. Whitey Ford was standing next to the wall. A photographer was setting up to take pictures. "I will treasure this moment forever," Glickman thought to himself.

The GM spoke first. "Steve, we really appreciate the time and effort that you gave us this season. You're a top-notch kid, a real gamer.

Unfortunately, you don't know enough about baseball to make a career with the Yankees organization. As a parting token, come over here and have your picture taken with George and Whitey. The picture will look good on the wall wherever you end up."

With that, Steinbrenner and Michael gave him a hug for the camera as if they were best friends. Whitey Ford stood in the background. Then, they walked out the door without a handshake, a pat on the back or even another word. Steve was so stunned that he had nothing to say.

Twenty-five years later, sitting in the stands as his team from East Timor thrashed Team Japan, Steve flashed back to this last Yankee meeting. "If I really don't know a thing about baseball, then how the fuck did my team just kick the shit out of Japan?" For emphasis, he chugged his fifth beer of the day.

Chapter 4

Garden Bostwick III, Guffy to his friends, grew up in Locust Valley, Long Island, New York. Hard working and brilliant, Guffy was tops in his class at Greenvale, a private elementary school, where the rich and famous sent their children. From there, he went on to St. Pauls and MIT. His family was so sure that he would complete the double play and join the family business on Wall Street that in his senior year of college they built and furnished an office for him in the Trinity Building in downtown Manhattan. Garden Bostwick III had other ideas. At first, he thought he wanted to be a cowboy. After sixteen years of formal education, he had had enough of the academic world and yearned for some real life adventures. However, after a couple of summers shoveling manure in other people's corrals, he changed his mind. He set his mind on working for the Walt Disney Company. With his degree in software engineering and his dry sense of humor, he decided that his dream job would be developing projects for Disney animation.

His MIT diploma was all the credential that he needed to be hired by Disney. Immediately, he was put on the fast track. Within five months, he sat in on meetings to screen new material. It soon became obvious that he was the rising star. It was his intuitive genius that led to the design and creation of Space Hoops, the movie in which cartoon characters recruit NBA stars to defeat space aliens in a basketball game to save the planet. Guffy not only approved the story, but he also edited the script and designed the softwarc to interface the animation with the real actors. Guffy's boss, Greg Jeffries, was a Disney lifer. Predictably, he took as much of the credit for the project as he could. Guffy didn't care. He was a team player and an idealist. "Do the right thing," he told himself, "and all will work out in the end."

Space Hoops opened in Los Angeles to rave reviews. An innovative concept, perfectly executed, the movie was an artistic and box office success. Guffy was becoming Disney's fair-haired boy. Lower level executives started to kiss his ass, and cute actress wannabes started to come on to him. When he looked at himself in the mirror each morning in his Oxford suits, he saw a deal maker. He knew that in a short time, he would be what the industry referred to as a player.

Guffy and Steve kept in close touch after they graduated. In fact, the day that Glickman was let go by the Yankees, Guffy was flying to New York in Disney's biggest jet for the New York premiere of Space Hoops. They agreed to meet at The Blue Dolphin for drinks after the premiere. The screening played to a full house of celebrities and media at Radio City Music Hall. The audience stood and cheered for every basket in the same way they applauded Rocky's KO of Apollo Creed. That night, Guffy got the biggest hand of all at the post-screening party. "Time to make the down payment on the Beverly Hills townhouse," he thought to himself.

The next day, he was called in to see Michael Eisner. "Bonus time," he thought. The CEO met him at the door of his Manhattan office which was bigger than most people's homes. They went through all the phony formalities of exchanging pleasantries, sharing one hundred-year-old cognac and Cuban cigars. After a suitable interval, Eisner started the discussion. "Young man you have great talent. Space Hoops is the hit that this company needed. However, our board of directors has decided to take the Disney Company in another direction. People have heard you saying some unkind things about me and other senior management. We don't care for your sense of humor. In fact, in some ways, you don't really have a sense of humor. We think it would be better for everyone if you found employment elsewhere."

Garden Bostwick III had just gone from fair-haired boy to sacrificial lamb in less than one minute. Months later, he would learn that Eisner had fired him because he was too smart and too funny to the point that Eisner felt threatened. He would never forget that meeting. In one respect, it had been quite an accomplishment to rise so quickly to the place that one of the most ruthless corporate hatchet men had disposed of him personally. Guffy would never forget the look in Eisner's eye when he uttered the words, "You are fired." Many a night, he would wake up in a cold sweat remembering how Eisner delighted in Guffy's pain all the while trying to appear kind and sympathetic.

That evening over drinks, the two college roommates decided to dedicate their lives to getting revenge.

Sitting by the foul pole with his friend as East Timor thrashed Japan, Guffy thought to himself, "I guess they will finally realize that I do have a sense of humor when the Major League all-stars have the shit kicked out of them by twelve clods named Snemelc Regor who look like they couldn't wipe the snot off their noses if they sneezed."

He stuffed another handful of peanuts in his mouth and downed it with a beer.

Chapter 5

Meanwhile, at the league offices in New York, the staff of Major League Baseball was scrambling. "Who are those guys?" was the question everyone was asking, and "Where did they come from?" The tabloids were full of theories. "Aliens from outer space" and "Ted Williams Clones" were some of the headlines. One of the papers claimed proof that the East Timoreans were direct descendants of Jim Thorpe and Babe Didrikson.

With game one of the series scheduled in a week, there were all kinds of logistical problems. Where could they get a recording of the East Timorean national anthem? Was there an East Timorean national anthem? What did the flag look like, etc., etc., etc.?

The greater problem facing Bud Selig was how to put a team on the field that could play ball with these creatures, whoever or whatever they were. Selig spent all day on the phone trying to recruit players. Many, like Barry Bonds, were not anxious to give up any of their vacation. They also were reluctant to mar their hero status on the chance that East Timor would win the series. "I would love to help out," Bonds said over the phone, "but I promised to play golf in the local benefit for the Red Cross. If there is a game three, give me a call. If something opens up on my schedule, I will keep you in mind."

Over and over, the commissioner was getting the same story. Some of the players that had committed to the games when they were expected to be pressure free exhibitions were backing out. There were some exceptions. Derek Jeter of the Yanks and Jason Varitek of the Red Sox called to say that they would play, but Selig wasn't sure he would be able to field a full team. Finally, out of desperation, he put in a call to an old friend. "If there was one person who might be able to pull something out of the hat, this was the guy who could do it," he thought to himself as he dialed.

"Hello," said the voice on the other end. "This is Tommy Lasorda."

Tommy Lasorda, the man who bled Dodger blue for 30 years, the man who had led an outclassed Olympic team to a gold medal in a thrilling victory over Cuba, the man who could motivate men and kids alike to walk through walls and swim oceans had been hoping that he just might get this call. Tommy had not managed a team for several years. He was seventy-five years old and out of shape but still lived and died for the game.

"Do you know why I am calling?" Bud Selig asked.

"I have a hunch that you need a manager for the series."

"Would you consider coming out of retirement?"

"I would love to," Tommy replied without a second of hesitation.

"Do you think that we would have a chance to beat these guys?"

"I haven't seen them play," was Tommy's response.

He paused for a moment. Then, using a line that he had used many times before, he said simply, "Americans invented baseball. We aren't going to let these donkeys beat us at our own game."

"How quick can you get to New York?" Selig asked.

"I will be on the red eye tonight. I'll start calling players from the air."

Selig wiped the sweat from his forehead, "Half of the job done." Now, he needed a general manager to help prepare the team. He turned to his assistant. "We need someone who is ruthless. We need a proven winner. We need someone who will stop at nothing to fight this enemy and defend our game. We need someone who has money and knows how to use it. We need someone who will do anything fair or foul, outrageous or vile to build a team with only victory in mind." His assistant didn't have to utter a word, but just nodded, and together they dialed George Steinbrenner.

"George," Bud Selig said. "I have Tommy Lasorda flying to New York to manage our team, but I need your help. We have got to find out what we are dealing with, and we have to figure out how to beat them. If you're in, you have my total and complete support."

George Steinbrenner was glad that the commissioner had called him. He knew the gravity of this series. Before the tournament had started, his estate planner had appraised the Yankees with a figure of $1.2 billion. He knew that if East Timor trashed the Major Leaguers, the value would be less than half of that. "I will do what I can to see that East Timor becomes famous for climbing mountains, or making pancakes or whatever the hell they do," George replied. "Have Lasorda come to the stadium as soon as he gets to town. I need to go now. The series starts next week, and I've got some serious preparations."

Selig hung up the phone still stressed but partially relieved. He now had baseball's top manager and top executive on his team.

Chapter 6

MIT, The Massachusetts Institute of Technology, was the college of choice for the brightest scientific and mathematical minds in the world. Not only were the students smart, but they were encouraged to be a little bit mischievous and rebellious. The college's thinking was that to a small degree, the lack of respect for institutions and conventions was an ingredient necessary to spark invention and foster progress. Many of the pranks designed on campus were the sheer genius of the famous scientists, inventors and engineers of the future.

When MIT students got peeved at other students, they didn't toilet paper their frat house. They built sound cannons to blow out dorm windows from across the quad. When teachers misbehaved, they didn't get nails in their tires. Students would break into their apartments and throw cryogenically frozen rats against their walls while they were on vacation, leaving them to break in thousands of pieces and rot in ninety-degree weather. Movie companies used to threaten MIT students who would access their servers and download feature movies the day they premiered. After a while, they gave up and quietly turned their backs, not wanting the publicity that their movies were so easily pirated. In fact, the reason that video voting machines were never accepted was that MIT students would have hacked the systems and elected all future presidents.

Many unexplained events were the work of student and alumni pranksters. One of Guffy's and Glickman's early acts of mischief occurred several years after graduation during the famous Yankee-Red Sox playoff series of 2003. The Red Sox, as a good will gesture put up for sale one hundred general admission seats on their website, first come first served. They were to go on sale at one o'clock sharp. Unbeknownst to anyone, MIT software engineers jammed the website at 12:59:58, allowing access to only their own computers. These super computers dialing at 200 times a second, bought all 100 tickets by 1:02 when the site was reopened. Guffy sold 95 of the tickets that he bought for $50 for $500 apiece. He made over $42,000 and went to the famous Don Zimmer-Pedro Martinez game for free. No one ever figured out what happened. The next day, The Boston Globe had a short article. "The website," the article read, "had some slight problems which team webmasters fixed promptly."

When Steve Glickman and Garden Bostwick III returned to campus the summer of 1981 after being fired, they had many enthusiastic friends anxious to help them plan their revenge. On a late summer night, at a coffee shop in Harvard Square, a team of biomechanics, quantum physicists, software engineers, geneticists, psychologists and chemists hatched a plan. The team's first idea was to design the perfect soldier and blackmail the world, but that had been done before in too many "B" movies. Besides, it wasn't their desire that anyone get hurt. Next, they discussed a plan to bankrupt Disney, but that wasn't humorous enough. The spirit of pranksterism demanded something more creative. Finally, they agreed on a plan to create the perfect ballplayer and make a mockery of America's national pastime. It was a fantasy project they could all sink their teeth into.

Chapter 7

When Tommy Lasorda's plane touched down at JFK, a driver and limo was waiting for him. "We will take your bags to your suite," the driver said. "Mr. Steinbrenner wants to see you at the stadium right away."

"I didn't bring any bags," Tommy replied. He was anxious to get to work. He had a productive flight. By the time he arrived, he had assembled his coaching staff and talked several players into volunteering. Like Eddie Jeremiah, the fabled hockey coach of Dartmouth lore, he never had to do heavy recruiting. The chance to play for Tommy Lasorda was an opportunity unto itself. Players didn't mind being awakened during the night to receive Tommy's call. Just like Little Leaguers waiting by the phone the night of all-star selections, many of the pros were sitting up hoping that they were on his list.

As soon as he got into the limo, Lasorda called Steinbrenner. In the past, neither man had much use for each other. Steinbrenner represented what Tommy hated about the game, big business with big money prostituting the game's purity and spiritual essence. Steinbrenner, who never liked to share the spotlight with anyone, was always jealous of Lasorda's love affair with the press and fans. Today, however, they were allies in a greater cause, protecting the stature and image of the game, and in spite of past petty quarrels, they did have tremendous respect for each other. They both knew that they were the best in the world at what they did.

"George," Tommy spoke into the cell phone, "we need to make arrangements for some players. David Ortiz and Curt Schilling are flying in from Boston. Johan Santana and Tori Hunter are coming in, too."

"Wonderful!" George replied. "My people are on it. Can you get over here right away? We are going to start a meeting, and I want you to meet my team."

Twenty-eight minutes later, Lasorda and his police escort arrived at "The Big Ball Park". How fitting that 'The House that Ruth built' would serve as the Alamo for baseball's last stand. Security whisked the old man up the elevator. Even though he was in his seventies and overweight, even though he had been up all night, Tommy had the energy of a twenty-year old. This was what he lived for.

As he walked into the room, Lasorda couldn't believe the faces sitting around the table. In the first seat to Steinbrenner's right sat Brian Cashman. In his early thirties, Cashman was a baseball genius. The current Yankee general manager, he would be in charge of logistics. Sitting to the Boss's left was Rudy Giuliani, the former mayor of New York and a great fan of the game. Rudy could be counted on to stay calm and think clearly. In his handling of the fallout after 9/11, Giuliani had proven his ability to fight enemies seen and unseen. If those three had been the only ones in the room, Lasorda would not have been surprised, but there were four more.

Next to the mayor, sat Jennifer Stone, the glamour queen. A former actress, she had parlayed her looks into fame and fortune, and then as if Hollywood stardom was not enough, she had become the Mata Hari of the gossip world. If there were young men involved with East Timor, there would be no secret safe from her sexuality.

Next to Brian Cashman sat Jim Grey, the television sports reporter. "What the fuck is he doing here?" Lasorda thought to himself. For most pro athletes, Jim Grey was the most annoying member of the ever-present press corps. Athletes were contractually bound to give interviews and talk to reporters. There was no one they hated talking to more than Jim Grey. At the Olympics, he routinely asked figure skaters if they would be able to handle the pressure. He would ask slumping batters if they thought they would ever hit again. As players got older, he would ask them if their age was catching up to them. There was no one better at planting doubt in an athlete's mind. If the press would be an ally against East Timor, he would be the leader of the band.

Next to him sat Dr. Lashman Singh, the world's most famous scientist and theoretician. Singh had developed a cult following as the man who could solve any puzzle, defeat any disease, outwit any foe. World leaders, wealthy celebrities, corporate CEOs would come to him for his wisdom whenever they had problems or dilemmas, and according to legend, possibly his own, he had never been stumped.

Most surprising was the last member of the group. At the far end of the table, wearing Dockers and tennis shoes, with two laptops in front of him, sat William Gates. Billy Gates, as he was better known, was the world's richest man. He had dropped out of Harvard to start Microsoft, one of the world's most successful companies. Possessed of a great mind and unlimited resources, he was, unbeknownst to most, a die-hard baseball fan. Furthermore, as the world's first and foremost self-described geek, he took umbrage to the East Timorean players for making fun of geeks and geekdom. Billy Gates had built his company by knowing how to think outside the box. When he interviewed engineers in Microsoft's early days, he didn't obsess about their resumes. Instead, he asked them why manhole covers were round. He was always less interested in academic genius than problem solving common sense. The man that would work for him would know that a round manhole cover could be rolled instead of lifted, and a round cover could not fall through a round hole.

Lasorda was impressed. In the quest of defending the American pastime against an unknown foe, the Yankee owner had assembled a dream team.

After brief introductions, George Steinbrenner spoke first. "Gentlemen, we have an important job to do. We must find a way to defeat East Timor." He threw in a little Winston Churchill for emphasis. "Never in baseball's long history, have so many depended on so few. Every little boy and girl with a bat and a mitt, is counting on us to help their heroes succeed. We cannot disappoint them."

He turned to Lashman Singh. "Mr. Singh, we would be honored if you would speak first."

Before the meeting had started, Professor Singh had insisted that he would be the first to talk, lest anyone would make any of his points before he had a chance to do so. The professor sported a long, grey beard and wore a big, red turban. He was wearing old, ratty pants and a dirty Cal Tech polo shirt. Before he spoke, he took a drink of water and cleared his throat twice. He adjusted his glasses and stared at the ceiling. "Laying it on a little thick," Billy Gates thought to himself. The professor began to speak in an annoyingly high-pitched voice.

Singh began. "We have a complex set of problems that can be solved with extensive algorithms." Most mathematical shamans used the word 'algorithm' liberally as it sounded quite brilliant, and very few people in an audience ever knew what it meant. A look at Billy Gates, who was getting annoyed because he did know what it meant, made him change his tack. "Remember," he said, "the hippopotamus has no stinger, but the wise man says tis better to be sat on by a bee than to be stung by a hippopotamus." He paused for a second waiting for his brilliance to be recognized. Disappointed that there was no applause, he continued. "My team from Cal Tech will analyze every inch of tape from East Timor's previous games. We will figure out everything that makes the players perform. We will discover their weaknesses. We will find their Achilles Heel. We will come up with strategies to make them weak and defeat them. We have no fear of failure. There is nothing that can be created at MIT that can't be destroyed by the superior minds at Cal Tech. With my assistants and technicians working around the clock, we will have the answer," he looked at his watch, "in three months at the latest."

There was silence in the room. No one had told the great Singh that the series started next Friday.

CHAPTER 8

George Steinbrenner quickly resumed command of the meeting. He spoke next to Jennifer Stone. "Ms. Stone, your powers of persuasion are unmatched." Jennifer started to blush. All of a sudden, George realized what he had said and started to blush, too. He changed the subject. "On the entry forms, we have determined that the team sponsors are two young men from MIT. They are in town for tomorrow's press conference. We have also found out that they are staying at the Park Avenue Regency. The last two mornings they have had power breakfast with their staff, and in the afternoon, they drink beer at the hotel bar. Get over there now and find out what you can. I want to know everything there is to know about them and more. What have they done for the last twenty years? What do they do for fun? Who they date, etc." He started to ask what color toilet paper they wiped their ass with, but decided that the line had been overused, and this was too solemn an occasion anyway.

Jennifer's face got sweet and perky. "I am on it boss," she said as she got up from the table. She was wearing the tightest, lowest cut dress. All of the men in the room watched her as she jiggled her way to the door. Billy Gates shot a look at Rudy Giuliani who then looked over at Tommy Lasorda, who then looked over to see George Steinbrenner staring at the voluptuous detective. After a couple of seconds, the dream team realized that they had all been caught peaking. They cleared their throats, shuffled some papers and resumed the meeting.

The Boss turned to Jim Grey. "Mr. Grey," he spoke in a serious manner, "you were briefed earlier this morning, and you have had a little time to prepare. What have you come up with? What can the press do to subvert the East Timor club?"

Jim Grey stood up and started talking. He was a short, efficacious man, universally despised by the sports establishment, but now, he was in his element. He was being asked by his prior enemies to be at his annoying and undermining best. "I have talked to some of the press corps. Most of the papers, TV and radio stations will help. We will hit East Timor with everything. Before the first pitch is thrown, each player will have to deal with a different set of distractions. Some will be asked if they are gay, if they gamble, or if they use steroids. Some will be asked if they beat their wife. Some will be asked if the rumors of stealing cookies from the girl scouts are true." Grey was getting warmed up almost to the point of frothing at the mouth. More surprisingly, the rest of the team, that usually detested his tactics, was enjoying being on the other side of the toilet. Grey continued, "I personally will ask the bench players, Snemelcs J., K. and L. if they suspect that they are not playing because of allegations of indecent behavior by management. Of course, we will play the whole pressure thing of performing in Yankee Stadium to the hilt. If anyone of them has anything to hide or be the least bit ashamed of, we will drag it out in front of the world, and if any of them has any animosity towards another teammate, we will exploit that also. We have spread some money around with hotel staff, clubhouse attendants and tour guides. There will be nothing that we won't discover or that will be too sacred to exploit. Naturally, I will be working closely with Ms. Stone to develop any intelligence that she uncovers." The thought of working with Jennifer Stone made Grey start to blush, and feeling the blood start to pump between his legs, he quickly sat down before he embarrassed himself.

"Thank you, Mr. Grey," the Boss said. "Rudy Giuliani will be my personal liaison with all the members of this team. He knows New York better than anyone, and he will make sure that everyone has the support and resources that they need. Isn't that right Rudy?" The ex-mayor nodded.

"Mr. Gates, thank you so much for your willingness to help us out. What can you tell us at this time?"

From his chair, Billy Gates started to talk. "I don't have enough data to analyze yet, so I don't have much to say, but," he hit a button on one of his laptops, and all of a sudden the lights in the room dimmed, and a screen dropped from the ceiling. The Microsoft logo flashed on a power point presentation, and the Star Wars theme came through the conference room speakers.

"How the fuck did he do that?" Steinbrenner thought to himself. All the other participants were impressed except for Lashman Singh. Singh was slightly peeved at being upstaged. He was used to being the number one tech guru.

Gates continued. "At this time, all I can say is that every system has a weakness." A rat appeared on the power point screen. "There is no system that can't be breached. My people will find the weak link. I have relieved five thousand engineers of all their duties to concentrate on this problem, and when we find it, which we will before next Friday," He shot a look at Professor Singh, whom he regarded as a quack, "we will find a way to crush it." On cue, a sledgehammer squished the rat on the screen, and guts flew in all directions. The room was stunned. None of them had realized that beneath his quiet, unassuming face, Mr. Gates had such a killer instinct. Apparently, the world's most benevolent philanthropist had a venomous hatred for those who made fun of geeks or who used technology towards evil ends.

George Steinbrenner had originally questioned Giuliani's recommendation to put Gates on the team, but now, he saw it as genius. Gates was a 'when they're down, kick them person'. "My type of guy," George thought to himself. "I just hope he doesn't like the Red Sox." He turned to Tommy Lasorda. Baseball's greatest ambassador was getting fed up with all the talk. "Enough of the bull shit," Tommy said. "Tomorrow morning the team starts to practice. We invented this game. We will beat the shit out of them on the field straight up."

Just then, a messenger walked in the room and handed Tommy a couple of notes. "Gentlemen," Tommy said reading the first note, "Albert Pujols is flying in from St. Louis and Vlad Guerrero is on his way from LA." He looked at the second note and beamed, "Doc Halladay is coming on the noon plane. The fight is just beginning."

With that, the meeting ended.

CHAPTER 9

Tuesday Afternoon

Jennifer Stone sat at the bar in The Park Place Regency Hotel. She had been there most of the day. The East Timor management had not shown up for breakfast. She had waited for almost two hours eating her eggs and sipping coffee while watching investment bankers click away at their Blackberrys making deals. The dealmakers wore white shirts, red ties and black oxfords, each one a spitting image of the next. She had lost count of how many times she had been hit on. Now, she sipped on a Virgin Bloody Mary. She had given the bartender the heads up that no matter what drink she ordered, he was to prepare it without alcohol. To say she was drop dead gorgeous was an understatement. She was wearing a low cut dress with spaghetti straps that left little to the imagination. At six-thirty, she noticed two men walk through the door and sit down at the corner table. A quick glance at the photo in her bag confirmed that they were her marks.

"Careful," she thought to herself, "don't be too obvious. Let them make the first move and then reel them in." After about twenty minutes of sucking on an empty glass and glancing in their direction, she finally made eye contact. Making it look like an accident, she spilled some peanuts down the front of her dress. Feigning embarrassment, she made a pretend attempt for privacy as she brushed the front of her breasts and reached in to remove the peanuts. Out of the corner of her eye, she noticed that she was getting their attention. She downed the final ice cube in her glass.

Steve Glickman finally bought what she was selling. Walking over very tentatively, he asked if she would like another drink. "Oh thank you, honey," Jennifer said in her sweetest Southern drawl.

"Why don't you bring it to our table," Glickman told the bartender.

Jennifer let Glickman take her hand and lead her to his table. "Total nerd," she thought to herself. "He probably has never been with a woman, especially one like me. This is going to be a piece of cake."

After the obligatory small talk and verbal foreplay, Jennifer asked, "What you little devils in town for?"

"We're here for the baseball series," Guffy replied.

"On my, but I do love baseball. Why, I had my first date at a Yankees game. It was a cold night, and I shared a blanket with my high school sweetheart. He was so frisky that..." Jennifer paused and blushed, "well you boys don't want to hear about that."

Watching Glickman's eyes, she could tell that he was smitten.

After a little more flirting, she brought the conversation around to the East Timor team.

Guffy made a lame attempt at a joke. "The most exciting game we played so far was beating West Timor in the Timorean playoffs. We had to beat them to qualify."

Jennifer chuckled and rolled her tongue slowly around her lips. "Tell me about your team. Who's your best player and is he married?" She reset her dress strap which had fallen over her shoulder.

Guffy tried to change the subject, but Glickman was on the hunt. "They all have equal talent. That's the beauty." Sensing his chance,

Glickman continued. "I have some great pictures of the boys up in my room. Would you like to see them?"

"Why, I would love to," Jennifer answered, and just like that, off they went.

Alone in the elevator, Jennifer pressed lightly against Glickman and stared into his eyes with the 'Oh, please kiss me look.' "I hear your boys have never been beaten. Are they the best players in the world?"

"The best that ever played," Glickman answered.

Jennifer didn't want to play her cards too quickly. She allowed herself to be kissed and melted into his arms. Trouble was that Steve Glickman didn't know how to kiss a girl much less hold her. It was very awkward. They got off the elevator and walked to his room.

"Tell me darling. Does your team ever lose? How can anyone beat them?"

"I can't wait to tell you, but first why don't you slip into something more comfortable?"

Glickman had waited forty years to use that line.

"Why I was just thinking about that myself," Jennifer replied.

After a few minutes, the detective emerged from the bathroom wearing only the black, see-through negligee that she had in her handbag. Glickman grabbed her and kissed her. He had no idea what he was doing, but he was doing it very aggressively. After a few wet kisses, Jennifer put her finger to his lip, "Oh darling, tell me how would anyone ever beat your boys. I need to get that off my mind so I can concentrate on making love."

Glickman kissed her on the check and stroked her hair. "There is only one thing that can beat them," he kissed her again and licked her ear. Jennifer giggled. "The only thing that can beat them," he whispered to her as he pulled her negligee down over her breasts, "is...," he paused "is kryptonite." He pushed her away and started laughing. Then he turned on the lights. His laughter became loud and uncontrollable. Standing half-naked in the middle of the room, Jennifer knew she had been played. She pulled up her negligee, threw her dress over her shoulder and stomped out of the room.

As she left, Glickman yelled after her, "Tell George that there is nothing that he's got that can beat my team, but if you want another drink, stop by tomorrow night after the press conference."

As Jennifer sped to the elevator half dressed, Glickman turned on the TV to catch Sportscenter. "What a moron," he thought to himself. "How could she think that I would fall for the honey babe routine."

In the elevator, Jennifer quickly dressed. She rummaged through her purse for her cell phone and punched a few numbers. She could hear Sportscenter and Glickman talking in the background. He had not noticed the bug that she had placed under his bed. "Men are such easy marks," she said out loud. Things had gone exactly as planned.

Chapter 10

Wednesday afternoon, The Press Conference:

George Steinbrenner, Rudy Giuliani and Billy Gates sat in George's office at Yankee Stadium. It was 1:45. They looked out the picture window onto the field. All the Major Leaguers were wearing smart red, white and blue warm-ups. As the week moved on, Tommy's recruiting effort had gained momentum. When heroes like Ken Griffey, Jr. and Randy Johnson signed on, no one wanted to be left off the best team ever assembled. With a few exceptions, the biggest names in the game were in town. George spent a few minutes watching Ichiro fire bullets from right field to home plate. He glanced over to the bullpen where Mariano Rivera and Eric Gagne were warming up. The world had never seen a team with anything near this talent. Tommy Lasorda was on the mound. In his younger days, he always threw thirty to forty minutes of batting practice. It was a habit, his signature. To this day, he still threw, but maybe only twenty or thirty pitches. The three men watched as his fastballs floated up to the plate. Ivan Rodriguez was hitting them well over the fence in deep center field. George commented how even a kid could knock those balls out of the park. Rudy nodded. Billy Gates was watching Lasorda, too. He seemed to be in deep thought and didn't say anything.

At 1:55, it was time to go downstairs to the pressroom. An overflow of reporters, all handpicked by Jim Grey were buzzing around. In a few minutes, they would be introduced to Steve Glickman, Garden Bostwick III and the players of the East Timor team. Following a brief statement and a few questions, George Steinbrenner and Tommy Lasorda would take the podium and talk about the Major League all-stars.

Billy Gates had been busy preparing for the press conference in a most unusual way. His first task was to gather genetic data on the East Timorean players. To that end, he arranged to have cans of coke on the podium for each player to drink. The idea was to analyze fingerprints after the conference to see if they were identical. In case they saw through this deception (he never underestimated his opponents), the table would also be covered with pictures to be autographed, another potential source of prints. At huge expense, he had equipped the security cameras around the room with special laser lens. Hopefully, they would be able to take retinal scans of all the players. He had flown in agents from the Griffin Agency in Las Vegas to supervise the project. The Griffin Agency was the elite company with the experience and know-how to identify and uncover the most notorious casino cheats. There was no one more qualified to see through any type of disguise. The cost of their services for a rush job was astronomical, but Mr. Gates picked up the tab personally. He wanted to win very badly, and after all, he was the richest man in the world.

The press conference got under way. Mayor Bloomberg and Bud Selig officially welcomed East Timor to New York and introduced the players. As they walked in, they were all wearing the same hideous uniforms, lime green and chartreuse. They were loud enough to block out the sun. Even Saul Stevens, the old, blind beat reporter for the

Tribune was stunned. The East Timor team sat in a row of chairs behind the podium. Their appearance conjured up the image of Jerry Lewis meets the Bride of Frankenstein. They had scruffy hair, unshaved faces, thick glasses, shirts hanging over their belts and big wads of chewing tobacco in the jaws. They sat in order, players number one to twelve, Snemelcs A. to L., each one a carbon copy of the other.

Garden Bostwick III took the podium first looking like the prep school freshman trying to win the prize for the ugliest clothes at the school prom. He was wearing a lime green blazer with the East Timor flag sewn on the pocket, chartreuse pants and a lime green tie. His hair was perfectly combed and parted, as if to ignore that the rest of his clothes were a crime against nature. His speech started generically. "It is a great honor to represent the world in this classic and to face the best players in the Major Leagues. We hope to make a fine showing." He abruptly changed gears. Turning to George Steinbrenner, he said, "It is too bad for baseball that the Major Leagues no longer have the best players. Countries like East Timor now field superior athletes. In a few years, no one will want to watch second-rate talent like the Yankees or Red Sox. They will have to travel far to see the premiere version of the game." He looked around and noticed that Steinbrenner was starting to fume. Brian Cashman was doing his best to keep the Boss from coming out of his chair. "Now," Guffy continued, "I don't have any prepared remarks other than to say that we expect to win easily and decisively. I don't expect this to be much of a contest. I would be happy to take a few questions."

Guffy's comments caught the press corps off guard. Jim Grey had arranged for shills in the audience to ask carefully prepared questions, such as, "Do the players feel abused by their coaches, and is it true that they could play successfully without amphetamines and steroids," but with the tone of Guffy's opening remarks, the reporters went into a frenzy looking for the real story. No one ever talked like that at a pre-game conference. All one normally said was how happy they were to be there and how much respect they had for the other team.

The first question was supposed to come from Anthony McCarren of the Daily News, but before he could speak, a reporter whom no one recognized stood up quickly. "I am Snort Koblish from the East Timor Sentinel, and I have just one question. How sure are you about winning this series?"

"Damn, these guys are good," Rudy Giuliani thought to himself. "Preempting our shills with their shills."

"Thank you for the question, Mr. Snort." Guffy adjusted his tie and looked George Steinbrenner right in the eye. "I am so sure that I am willing to make a little wager, even though I don't expect anyone to have the guts to accept it." After a slight pause and still starring at Steinbrenner, he continued. "I saw you quoted in the press when this tournament started, that no amateurs could stay on the field with a Major League team, much less all-stars. If you really mean that, and you are willing to back it up, I would propose this simple wager. If your team wins as easily as you say they will, we will turn over all of our research for developing the perfect athlete to the commissioner's office, and The East Timorean government will pay you $500,000,000."

Glickman sat down. Quickly Snort Koblish stood up. "What happens if you win?"

"Oh, I almost forgot," Glickman replied. "If in, as George says, the unlikely event that our amateurs beat the all-stars, I only want one thing. I want controlling interest in the New York Yankees." With a bored look on his face, Glickman sat down again.

Brian Cashman had been afraid that something like this might happen. As George Steinbrenner jumped out of his seat, Brian reached for his belt to try to hold him back, but he was too late. Steinbrenner charged to the podium. "Mr. Bostwick," Steinbrenner shouted into the mike before he had time to think, "I would be happy to accept your proposition, but let's make it a little more interesting. I will throw in another $500,000,000 of my own money." Flash bulbs started to go off, and cameras started to click. "A billion dollars says that my team of major league all-stars will beat your rag tag bunch of water boy wannabes." Then, realizing what he had just done Steinbrenner turned white and flopped into a chair.

Guffy quickly accepted the wager. Baseball's goodwill tourney had just turned into a $1,000,000,000 boondoggle.

CHAPTER 11

Final Preparations:

When Team MLB, as they had started to call themselves gathered in the Yankee boardroom Thursday afternoon, the mood was far more somber than the first meeting. This was no longer fun and games. In fact, with one billion dollars at stake, this was the biggest money sports series in history. Las Vegas was getting more action than for the last Superbowl, and the early odds were three to two in favor of East Timor. There was a second line established at some of the casinos, even money, that George Steinbrenner did not have the $500,000,000 to make good on his bet if he lost.

After all the members of the team arrived, Brian Cashman called the meeting to order. Sitting at the table were Giuliani, Singh, Stone, Grey, Lasorda and Gates. George sat in a chair back in the corner. He had a pale, nauseated look on his face. Cashman was all business. "The series starts tomorrow, gentlemen. You have all had two days to gather intelligence and put together your reports. What do you have for us? Professor Singh, the floor is yours."

Lashman Singh stood up slowly, buttoned his jacket and paused to give his presentation the necessary drama. He pushed a key on his laptop. The lights dimmed and two screens dropped from the ceiling. It seemed that since Bill Gates had used one screen, not to be outdone, he needed two. On the first screen, against a fiery crimson background, three capital letters SSS appeared. The first S moved to the top of the screen and morphed into the word 'Science'. After a couple of seconds, the powerful music from 2001 a Space Odyssey blared through the room's speakers. Then, the second S moved below the word 'Science' and transformed into the word 'Solutions'. As the music hit a crescendo, the third S changed into the word 'Singh'. On the screen in fiery red letters, were the words Science, Solutions, SINGH. 'Singh' was three times as big as the first two words. Simultaneously, on the second screen, a collage of pictures of the great scientist flashed one after the other. The collage showed Singh in different outfits and in different forums accepting acclaim for some of his previous accomplishments.

Then, the professor spoke. His voice was more high-pitched and irritating than ever. "My fellow colleagues, before I start, I want you all to remember that an oak tree is just a nut that held its ground. We have seen through many of the mysteries of East Timor. For one thing, did any of you in this room realize that Snemelc Regor is really Roger Clemens spelled backwards?" He paused, waiting for the applause that surely should have accompanied such a stunning revelation. After a few seconds of silence, he continued, "Secondly, my people have determined without a shadow of a doubt that the East Timor players are all clones." He waited for more applause, but the silence continued. Speaking first, he knew he could take credit for all the obvious conclusions before Billy Gates got the floor. "Now, the secrets of beating this team are less obvious, but still very direct. We must build better clones. We must have access to stem cell research. We must find out the genetic material that their scientists have used for their source.

I assure you that my team of scientists will work on this nonstop until we have the answers. Regardless of the outcome of this first series, we will have superior talent by next year. In the meantime, I plan to personally watch every side and every bowl of every contest," the professor was getting his baseball terms mixed up with cricket, "until I have discovered every one of their secrets."

The professor hit another key on his computer. Now, on both screens, the letters, SSS flashed alternatively with the words, Science, Solutions, Singh. The 1812 Overture boomed through the speakers, and simulated fireworks began to explode. Singh looked over at an angry Billy Gates. "That should upstage the little fart," Singh thought to himself.

"Thank you professor," Brian Cashman said wondering whose idea it was to invite an Indian mystic to help run a baseball team. "Mr. Grey, you are next."

Jim Grey stood up with an apologetic look on his face. "I am sorry guys," he said. "We had all kinds of questions prepared for the press conference, but things got out of hand after the wager. We were ready to jump on their players at the workout this morning, but East Timor didn't show up. We haven't had access to any of the team. We don't even know where they are staying. It's almost like they don't trust the press corps."

The stupidity of the last remark was about to solicit a response from Steinbrenner, but before he could say anything, Jennifer Stone cut in. "Gentlemen, don't ask me my source, but the players are staying at Motel Six, Coney Island. They are spending their days playing video games and doing cannonballs into the hotel pool. They are acting like a bunch of sixth graders running around and sneaking peaks at the ladies on the beach in their bikinis. The players are so geeky that it seems to me, they are trying to make a mockery of this whole event."

Billy Gates bristled at the use of the word, geek. Jennifer Stone continued. "I have planted some bugs that I am pretty sure they are not aware of. I don't have anything else yet, but I am still analyzing some of the hotel room conversations. Let me know if there is anything specific that any of you are looking for, and I will see what I can come up with.

"Tommy, how is the team looking?" Cashman asked.

Tommy Lasorda stood up. He wasn't the least bit shy. As always, his persona radiated confidence and enthusiasm. "Guys, the all-star team representing our side is the greatest compilation of baseball talent ever assembled. They are dead serious. They don't appreciate those two MIT castoffs making a joke of this series. I have never watched East Timor play, but they better be ready because my boys are going give them everything they got and more. If I was a gambling man, I wouldn't bet against our team."

Lasorda sat down. Even though there was doubt and uncertainty in the room, there was one thing that everyone absolutely agreed on. There was no one in the world more suited to lead the team than Tommy Lasorda.

"Mr. Gates, it's your turn. What do you have to say?"

Billy Gates walked to the front of the room. This time he had no computers, music or video in his presentation. He was wearing the same clothes that he had on yesterday. It was obvious that he had not gotten much sleep. It was also obvious that he was growing increasingly angry at everything East Timor. The gawking players, the ugly uniforms, their total lack of respect for anything and everything all in the name of a sick joke was giving science and technology a bad name.

"Professor Singh is right. Our consultants have confirmed that all the Snemelcs are genetically identical. Whether or not they are clones is a different discussion that no one is interested in at this time." Singh glowed. It was not the average person that got a compliment from Mr. Gates. Singh started to add something, but Gates cut him off. It was not that Gates had no sense of humor, but at this time, he was in no mood to be amused.

Chapter 12

Billy Gates continued, "The first thing we need to find out is if we can beat them straight up. Tommy, I hope you are right, but we have to be realistic. East Timor beat up on Korea and Japan like they were a bunch of little leaguers. We have agreed that in this series there will be no mercy rule. If we get behind in the first game, I have designed a few experiments that might help us in games two and three. Since we know the players are clones, we need to deal with this as a behavioral problem. Who they are is less important than how they are programmed."

As he talked, it was apparent to those around the table that this man emanated genius. Everyone found themselves spellbound by his analytical proficiency, everyone, that is except for Professor Singh who pretended to clap enthusiastically, but was actually despondent at playing second fiddle. He was thinking less about the upcoming series and more about upstaging Gates the next time he spoke.

Gates outlined several experiments designed to develop intelligence on the opposition's players. To the richest man on the earth, who was not able to spend or give away his fortunes, this was a special challenge. Whatever it cost, he was determined to save the world from evil scientists.

When Gates was finished, there was a short discussion. Afterwards,

George Steinbrenner stood up to propose a toast. Speaking for the first time in the session, the Boss was not his usually boisterous self. He spoke softly but was still resolute. "Gentlemen, we have been brought together to face a monumental challenge. History will remember us as defenders of this great game against those who would make it a big joke for their own selfish purpose. Every Little Leaguer in the world will be watching their heroes fight this great dragon. We must do all in our power to help their heroes. We must not fail. Gentlemen, raise your glasses to the great game of baseball."

Brian Cashman had been with Steinbrenner for many years. During that time, he, like everyone else, sometimes saw his boss as a caricature of the wealthy industrialist that wielded the big bankroll to steamroll all in his way. Today, as he listened to George make the impassioned toast with a tear in his eye, he was never prouder to work for him and be a member of the New York Yankees.

The meeting adjourned, and the group headed home. Tomorrow would be a big day.

CHAPTER 13

Friday Morning: Let the games begin.

Yankee Stadium was built in 1918 to be the grand stage. It was the Mecca that at least once in their youth, every child within miles would make a pilgrimage to. There were many parks where one could watch a ball game, but there was only one Yankee Stadium. If the stadium was the shrine, Monument Park behind center field, was the Holy Grail. In Monument Park, a wall of plaques immortalized the great heroes of the past, Ruth, Gehrig, Dimaggio, Mantle. When visiting teams made their first trip to 'The Stadium', they would always spend a few minutes strolling through Monument Park to pay their respects. When Cashman and Steinbrenner arrived at the stadium that day, they were surprised to see East Timor in Monument Park during the time allotted for their batting practice. They watched with disgust as the players took pictures holding rabbit ears over the Babe's bust, and pretended to smooch the bronze of Mickey Mantle. "What a sacrilege," Steinbrenner thought to himself. "Jennifer Stone was right. East Timor was not interested in just winning. They wanted to make a mockery of the game."

Cashman was more succinct. "They want to shit on everything special."

Meanwhile, in the home clubhouse, Tommy Lasorda was filling in his lineup card. Following Bill Gates' suggestions, they had enacted some special rules for the series. The teams were allowed an unlimited roster of players. The mercy rule was abolished, and several other rules were enacted to commemorate the occasion. At the press conference to announce the changes, Glickman had agreed to every request, his motive obvious, to make it look like he was showing mercy on the Major Leaguers. If the all-stars lost, there would be no excuses.

Tommy Lasorda was right when he declared that the world had never seen a better collection of baseball talent. Ichiro would lead off and play right field. Derek Jeter, the Yankees' captain, batted second playing shortstop. He would be followed by Alex Rodriguez playing third. The cleanup hitter would be the designated hitter, David Ortiz. Following Ortiz would be Albert Pujols at first, Vlad Guerro in left, Andrew Jones in center and Ivan Rodriguez behind the plate. Jose Reyes, the Mets sensational rookie shortstop had agreed to move to second base. He would bat ninth. No team had ever seen the power, the speed, and the defensive prowess. Curt Schilling would get the ball for game one. Lurking in the bullpen would be the likes of Jonathan Papelbon, K-Rod, Flash Gordon and of course the greatest closer of all time, Mariano Rivera.

Before the team left the clubhouse, Tommy Lasorda's remarks were short and simple. "Fellas, we have played in a lot of big games before, but this is The Real World Series. Most of you don't know where East Timor is, but they have been disrespectful of you, our countries, our institutions and the game itself." Tommy paused for a second and then concluded as only Tommy could. "I want you to kick the shit out of them."

As game time approached, every seat in the big ballpark was filled. They could have sold out three times. There was standing room only for people who stood in line all night. The game was to be broadcast live to every baseball country in the world. The all-stars took the field. Curt Schilling finished his warm up tosses, touched his cross and the umpire yelled play ball. Snemelc A. Regor strode toward the plate.

CHAPTER 14

Game one of the three game series was essentially over by the third inning. The score was East Timor 9, Major League All-stars 1. The Snemelcs hit five home runs. It was apparent to all knowledgeable fans that they could have hit several more. Curt Schilling gave it a game effort on the mound, but nothing that he could throw; fastball, slider or changeup fazed the East Timorean batters. The all-stars lone score came on a solo home run by David Ortiz, who put a marvelous swing on what the replay showed to be an unhittable slider from Snemelc J. Other than that, the all-star batters went down anemically in order. In the owners box, George Steinbrenner and Brian Cashman watched the game without emotion. They were correct in their thinking. East Timor wanted to win decisively. They also wanted to embarrass the home team, but they didn't want to beat them so badly that the fans would feel sorry for them. That was a fine line that they wouldn't cross. Show them up for the overpaid prima donnas that they were, but don't turn them into martyrs, not yet anyway. A fight almost started in the top of the third. Snemelc K. rounded third and waltzed into a tag at home plate, making it obvious that he was running into an out so as not to run up the score. That was the ultimate insult and the last straw as far as Pudge Rodriguez was concerned. The catcher applied the tag high and hard. There might have been trouble had not Derek Jeter and some other calm heads prevailed. "We have two games left," Derek told Pudge even though he didn't know if the series would go a full three. A disconsolate Steinbrenner had the same thought. He wondered if this might be his last two games in the owners box.

In the middle of the fourth inning, Billy Gates summoned Tommy Lasorda to the clubhouse. Gates didn't come into the dugout as he did not want to be seen. When Tommy arrived, a red-eyed Gates was standing next to the water cooler with a clipboard and some papers.

"Tommy, I know that you haven't given up, but it looks like an uphill battle. I don't think that we can take the chance that our boys will adjust. We need to figure out East Timor's weaknesses, and I need you to get me some data." He handed Lasorda some papers. Here is a list of experiments you need to run in the next few innings."

Tommy Lasorda looked white. Part of him wanted to tell Gates to get out of the clubhouse and give him more time, but he knew that Gates was right. There was too much riding on the series. Tommy would never give up, but this was more of a technological problem than a baseball one. He needed the genius' help. He took a quick look at the papers that Gates handed him, shrugged his head and headed back to the dugout.

Tommy started the experiments immediately. Derek Jeter led off the fourth inning. To everyone's surprise, Jeter, a right-handed batter walked over to the left-handers batting box. Even more surprising, he set up batting right handed with his backside to home plate. Snemelc looked confused. The first pitch would have been a perfect strike, knee high except that it sailed in front of Jeter instead of over the plate. The next three pitches were identical, rolling to the backstop, giving Jeter a free pass. The pitcher looked confused. Billy Gates watched with interest. After every pitch, he banged away at his computer. The crowd started cheering. Maybe there was some hope for the home team yet. In his box, Steinbrenner cracked a small smile. The smile was short lived. When A-Rod, the next batter tried the same stunt, Snemelc's first pitch came right over the plate. With an eight-run lead, the game became a sideshow. The all-stars, proud athletes, did not take the beating lightly, and they were not happy with the stunts that Lasorda had them perform, but perform them they did out of respect for their manager.

In the top of the fifth, the umpires presented Johann Santana who was now pitching for the stars, a red baseball. East Timor protested until tournament officials showed them the rule allowing special commemorative baseballs that would be sent to the Hall of Fame after the series. Johann struck out Snemelc G. rather easily. The batter didn't seem to be able to judge his swing. The crowd starting cheering, but alas, the next batter quickly adjusted with a long easy home run. In the fifth inning, Gates arranged for five rats to be let loose in East Timor's dugout. He watched through his binoculars making copious notes on the players' reactions. The tests continued. Pujols swung before the pitcher pitched the ball. Similar result, a walk followed by a strikeout to the next batter. Santana did double and triple windups before releasing the ball. Jason Giambi, pinch-hitting, went to bat with a pool cue. In the next inning, the stars moved all their fielders to the left side of the diamond and then the right. The experiments continued one after another, each one zanier than the next. The big score board in center field flashed all sorts of pictures and messages all hoping to get East Timor's attention and distract their players. The last test had B. J. Ryan, the stars final pitcher try to bounce the ball through the strike zone. As crazy as the tests were, some of them produced positive results. Still, no matter what the test, East Timor quickly adjusted. When Pujols made the last out in the bottom of the ninth, the final score was East Timor 15, All-stars 2.

In the stands, Glickman and Guffy were living it up. Their entourage of rappers, hookers and “A” list wannabes took up two sections of box seats. They were having a wild time, downing beers, playing kissy-face with the girls and shouting insults at the umpires. By contrast, a discouraged George Steinbrenner kicked the trash can across his office and left without saying goodbye to anyone. He left through the same door that he and Gene Michael had used after firing Glickman many years ago.

As the crowd wandered out, scalpers tried to hawk tickets for Saturday’s game. However, tickets, which would have fetched $500 three hours ago, were finding no takers at five bucks a piece.

Chapter 15

East Timor 48 hours earlier:

East Timor, officially the Democratic Republic of Timor-Leste, was a country in Southeast Asia comprising the eastern half of the island of Timor located north of Australia. One of the poorest countries in the world, East Timor was colonized first by Portugal and then by Indonesia. It became independent in 2002. East Timor was known primarily for sandalwood and coffee until recently, when oil was discovered in the territorial waters.

Wednesday morning, just before dawn, Billy Gates' personal Gulfstream 4, christened Windows 1, landed at the airport in Dili, the nation's capital city. As the plane taxied to the terminal, the airport started buzzing as very few private planes landed at Dili even though it was the nation's only international airport. By the time the plane reached the gate, the word had reached the streets of the city that the plane of the world's richest man was sitting on the tarmac.

No one could have guessed what a strange, eclectic group sat inside the plane and what was their even stranger purpose.

The plane carried an assault team. Their mission was to gather information and intelligence leading to the subversion and destruction of Team East Timor. The leader of the team would be Rudy Giuliani. Gates had put him in charge counting on his political experience and pragmatism. Traveling with the team were George and Yaunchy, interpreters fluent in both Portuguese and Tetum, the native language of East Timor. Giuliani had also enlisted two friends, Tiger Woods and Tom Cruise. Icons recognized all over the world, they were along to win friends and gain influence with the local population. Paris Hilton completed the assault team for obvious reasons. They were supported by three photographers, a traveling secretary and ten of Microsoft's best all purpose technicians. Just like the pilgrims, who brought trinkets to trade with the Indians and the Bengal Lancers that conquered India using primarily beads, the hold of the plane was full of IPods, laptops, autographed photos, golf balls and other elements of cultural warfare. Not to mention, the team had a war chest of over ten million dollars in small bills as "tokens of appreciation" to be used as needed.

After deplaning, the assault team proceeded to customs. East Timor's lone custom official was so stunned by the celebrity of the visitors that he allowed them to pass without inspection. For his efforts, he was given a poster of Mission Impossible III signed by Mr. Cruise. The message was simple. There would be many goodies for anyone that cooperated.

It didn't take long for that word to spread. One hour later, the team had rented every car at the airport and hired native guides as drivers. The first contact outside the airport was a young man in his early thirties. A promise of a trip to the Casbar, the local hot spot nightclub, to party with Paris Hilton was all that was needed to loosen his tongue. "I know why you are here," he pronounced. "The answers to all your questions can be found at The Timor Institute of Technology and Sports." He gave the group directions to the Institute, or "TITS" as it was called, took Paris by the hand and headed into town.

Giuliani knew that he was off to a good start. "This is almost too easy," he thought to himself. It was time to start the expedition. After the technicians assembled the satellite phones and attached antennas to the rental cars, the caravan proceeded on the one road out of town, heading up to the mountains.

As they drove up the winding roads, the team couldn't help admiring the beauty of the small villages and well groomed fields. They also noticed the poverty of naked children and malnourished beggars. "A strange country to be developing world class sports teams," Tiger remarked, "and I haven't seen one baseball diamond."

At three in the afternoon, they arrived at the gate of the Timor Institute. It was manned by two armed guards that stopped the procession and asked to see some papers. Like Delta Force, the fabled assault team of almost every B movie, the players sprung into action. This time, instead of Chuck Norris and his ninjas throwing Shuriken stars, Cruise and Woods handed out bobble head dolls. In a flash, the team stormed the gates and proceeded to recognizance of the facility. From atop an adjoining hill, they looked down on fields of baseball diamonds. Scientists in lab coats were walking around with clipboards watching hundreds of Snemelc Regors batting, running and shagging flies. There was only one thing left to do. First, it was time to synchronize their watches.

Chapter 16

A large, multi-level building stood next to the fields. Giuliani looked at the guards by the front door and guessing that the building might house computers and records, he decided to order a diversionary tactic. He sent Tiger, Tom Cruise, two photographers and a secretary down to the field. Bingo! In a short time, all the East Timor players and coaches were gathered around having their pictures taken with the icons.

The ex-mayor proceeded with phase two. When the guard at the door stopped them and asked to see their credentials, Rudy filled his fist with $100 bills. "Official business!" he exclaimed. The guard looked at the pile of money in his hand. "Please enjoy your stay," he instructed them. The team entered the facility.

Once inside, things got sticky. Most of the workers seemed loyal to the cause. No one offered any information. It was time for Giuliani's political skills to kick in. He knew that in an organization of this size, there had to be at least one disgruntled employee. No matter how happy and secure the workforce, there would be one poor soul that could be turned. Fifty IPods later he hit pay dirt. In the computer lab, Rudy struck up a conversation with a technician whose nametag read Werner. Werner was wearing a pocket protector with the letters RPI, which Rudy knew stood for Rensselaer Polytechnic Institute. Knowing that

RPI grads resented the superior reputation of MIT, the former mayor fired a volley. "How does anything run in a place that's managed by pricks from MIT?" he asked. One look in Werner's eyes told him that he had found his mole.

After several minutes of stroking his ego, Giuliani got what he wanted. Werner confided to the mayor that he felt overworked and underappreciated. Giuliani was the epitome of the warm sympathetic listener. Werner told him detail after detail of Project "ETY" which stood for East Timor Yankees. He even offered to share a copy of the data files and the special video that Glickman and Bostwick had produced to promote the obligatory made for TV movie. Rudy recorded every word on the specially modified Blackberry that Billy Gates had given him. As Werner talked, Rudy looked out of the window down onto the fields. He couldn't help smiling. Tiger was conducting a clinic hitting golf balls to within inches of first, second and third base in front of a gawking audience. The people that weren't watching him were gathered around Tom Cruise who was putting on an exhibition demonstrating his karate moves from Mission Impossible III and taking staged pictures in pretend combat with the many Snemelc Regors.

After about an hour, Rudy had what he needed. It was time to extricate Delta Force. He tapped a radio button in his pocket to signal retreat. The team assembled back to their staging area. Tiger and Cruise were ecstatic. Tiger had enjoyed the company of the world-class athletes, and Cruise had converted several of his newfound friends to Scientology. The team loaded their vehicles with the data disks and laptops that they secured and headed back to town.

Paris Hilton was waiting for them when they arrived at the airport.

Unfortunately, the head of East Timor customs was waiting too. Someone from the presidential palace had reminded the officials that East Timor had $1,000,000,000 riding on the outcome of the series. The official insisted that they inspect all of the team's belongings before giving permission to take off. Thinking quickly, Tiger Woods threw his golf bag onto the tarmac. Following his cue, Cruise heaved his autographed photos in a different direction. Giuliani took what was left of his money and tossed the bills up into the air. Bedlam followed. The crowd that had gathered overwhelmed the small security detail and swarmed the tarmac. The authorities thought they had the crowd contained until Paris Hilton tossed her bra into the mass. The police lost control. Giuliani's Raiders beat a hasty retreat back to the plane. The pilots had the engines running, and before anyone could stop them, they headed down the runway and took off. As they looked back to the ground, they could see that East Timor's finest had found some weapons and were firing at the plane. The passengers had mixed emotions. On the one hand, no one felt comfortable being fired at. On the other hand, it was pretty exciting to have pulled off the mission and be safely in the air. Of all the team members, Tom Cruise was the most excited. He had a big smile on his face as he shook everyone's hand. It was easy to understand why. After twenty some years of playing this role in movie after movie, he had finally been a part of the real thing. Truth was indeed better than fiction.

CHAPTER 17

Yankee Stadium Saturday morning:

George Steinbrenner sat at the head of the big table in the Yankees' boardroom with his special advisors. All of the members of the team were there with the exception of Bill Gates. As they waited to start the meeting, the mood was somber. They had lost game one in a big way, and game two would be starting in a couple of hours. He looked at the photos on the wall of the Babe, Reggie Jackson and Joltin Joe Dimaggio. Afraid that he might be looking at them for the last time, Steinbrenner felt the worst of all. The Yankees were the greatest dynasty in the history of sports. He didn't want them to be dismantled under his watch.

Finally, Gates arrived. He was still wearing the same clothes from last Monday morning, and there were bags under his eyes. He brought a guest with him to the meeting, a man in his mid forties wearing a drab grey suit. Between them, they carried three backpacks of papers and assorted devices. They sat down at the end of the table under the famous photo of the dying Lou Gehrig giving his 'luckiest man on the face of the earth' speech.

Tommy Lasorda didn't wait to be called on. "Fellas," he said, his voice choking with shame, "we can't beat these guys straight up. I need whatever help you can give me. I have nothing more to say." In his fifty years as baseball's ambassador, no one ever remembered Tommy Lasorda speechless or with a defeatist tone in his voice.

Lashman Singh spoke next. As he arose, Jennifer Stone noticed that the grey in his long curled beard was smudged. "That asshole must dye his beard," she thought to herself. Singh walked to the blackboard in the front of the room. He was wearing his usual mystic garb with the exception that his turban had a Yankee insignia on the front. "Gentlemen," he started, "we cannot let ourselves get down. We must stay upbeat and optimistic. To that goal, I have made you all a gift. Please open the basket in front of you. You will see many items including a video of various global problems solved by the Singh organization. I hope this will provide the motivation to continue. You will also be getting a coffee mug with my logo, a specially designed Swiss Army Knife and an engraved four in one combination screwdriver. I hope these small gifts will inspire your creativity." Singh started to continue, but Billy Gates had had enough. The usually pacifist entrepreneur had been up for five days in a row. With game two starting soon, he knew that time was precious. He charged Professor Singh and grabbed him by his beard. Brian Cashman quickly separated the two combatants. Singh was shaken, and Gates immediately felt foolish. Cashman sat Singh down and handed him a glass of water. "Please take a minute to compose yourself, Professor," he said.

Gates wiped the sweat of his chin and took charge of the meeting. "I don't mean to be rude," he started, "but if all of you will sit down and listen, I think I might know how to beat these bastards." He wiped his glasses and continued. Having studied the data from Mr. Giuliani's trip and the experiments that were performed in game one, we know the following about our adversaries. The Timor Institute of Technology and Sports," Gates decided to refer to the institute by its full name instead of the more vulgar acronym, "has downloaded every Major League game in recorded history into their computers. They have analyzed every pitch of every inning. Their players have been programmed to anticipate every tendency, and in spite of their deceiving appearance, they are world-class athletes. On the videos that Rudy brought back, we have seen them perform physical feats that you would not believe. Trust me, there is no way you can beat them head to head. We also know that when they are confused by situations that they have not been programmed for, they can quickly adjust and make the necessary corrections. Due to intelligence gathered by the bug that Jennifer planted in Steve Glickman's room, we have determined that technicians from the Timor Institute can communicate with the players through tiny receivers in their eyeglasses."

Lashman Singh who had now regained his composure interrupted, "Just as I suspected, that means that if..."

Gates cut him off, "Please Professor, let me continue. We have designed a game plan that just might throw enough wildcards at them to steal game two. Because of their ability to make adjustments, we cannot use the same gambit twice. If we are going to have a chance to win the series, we must also be able to infiltrate and scuttle their systems. At this time, I would like to introduce to you Mr. Peter Norton. Peter is the founder of Norton Antivirus and Norton tools. If there is a way to hack into their systems, Peter Norton is the man who can do it.

Norton stood up next to the billionaire. "Gentleman, I will get right to the point. We know that they communicate, but we do not know their frequency. We also suspect that they are using 100,000 bit encryption to protect their data. My task is straightforward but extremely complicated. We must figure out where the communications are being transmitted from and what channels they are using. We must debug the encryption, break the code, and figure out how to transmit flawed instructions to the players. If you can throw enough curveballs at them in game two," Norton was proud of himself for using a baseball analogy, "to where they must do multiple transmissions, we have a chance to bust their systems. Normally, this type of infiltration would take weeks or months, but we have a special asset. The director of NASA is a friend of mine and a baseball fan. He has put the entire resources of their facility at my disposal. Their computers can do 100,000,000 calculations per second. Your job," he looked over his glasses at Tommy Lasorda, "is to win game two and give us the time to hack into their systems for game three. My senior associate, Tankai Lu, the foremost mathematician in the world, will personally supervise the effort."

The team members were getting excited, and energy was building until the Boss spoke somberly, "But guys, how are we going to win game two?"

"We have a plan," Bill Gates answered back. "I won't tell you all the details because we haven't worked them out yet, but I will tell you this. Our starting pitcher will be Tim Wakefield."

There was silence in the room.

"Tim Wakefield instead of Doc Halladay. You must be crazy. He is forty-two years old, and he hasn't won a big game in years," George shouted.

"We know," Gates replied, "but he throws a knuckleball. The science behind a knuckleball has never been quantitatively explained. Everyone is unique and unpredictable. Different air currents and temperatures make them break in different directions. The key word is unique. They will develop algorithms to decipher it eventually," He looked at Singh who seemed peeved that Gates had absconded with his word, "but it will buy us some time, maybe a few innings. In the meantime, we have some ideas for stealing a run or two. Anyway, it's the best chance we have, maybe the only chance. Now, we have to get going. We have little time left to set up our equipment and brief our players."

With that, the meeting adjourned. Gates said a couple of words to George Steinbrenner and gave him a pat on the back. As he walked out, he tossed his bag of Singh memorabilia into the trash can by the door. Looking down, he noticed that the can was already full of Singh mugs and engraved billfolds.

Chapter 18

Yankee Stadium Game Two:

Long before a single fan crossed a turnstile, Billy Gates and Peter Norton were busy with their special preparations. First, all the gates were equipped with modified metal detectors. The hope was to confiscate computers, radios or transmitters that might provide access to East Timor's network. Special FBI Agent, Smoky Hines, was in charge of security details at each gate. Elaborate profiles had been established to identify operatives of the East Timor team. Meanwhile, Gates and Norton personally supervised the installation of bugging and jamming equipment in all corners of the ballpark. At the same time, a team led by off duty secret service operatives swept the entire stadium hoping to find any contraband that might have been hidden by Glickman's or Bostwick's organization.

The gate detail was the first to hit pay dirt. A ninety-year-old lady bringing her grandkids to the game set off a metal detector. Searchers found an ultra thin lap top sewn into her coat. When questioned, she said that a nice young man had asked her to deliver it to some box seats behind third base. Smoky Hines ordered the computer sent to the temporary tech lab set up in the bomb shelter underneath the stadium. He assigned an undercover agent to accompany the lady to her rendezvous.

In the tech lab, hastily built in the bowels of the stadium, a crew of FBI scientists tore into the laptop. The firewall seemed no match for NASA's engineers. Just when they were beginning to make progress, a strange noise started emanating from the machine. It started quietly and then amplified to a frightening squeal. The agents, afraid that the device was booby trapped, started to run when suddenly the noise stopped and a half naked stripper appeared on the screen. "Hi boys," the stripper teased in a suggestive voice. "I bet you thought you were pretty good." She proceeded to remove what was left of her clothing. "By the time you watch this, your team will have lost game two. Now, you can kiss my rear end." The screen went blank. There was a loud pop, and smoke started coming from the fried processor.

"Damn them," said Smoky, "what a bunch of irreverent bastards."

Gates and Norton were disappointed when they heard the news, but they weren't surprised.

Meanwhile, in the umpires room, the equipment boys under Gates' supervision were replacing the official baseballs with several batches of 'special commemorative' ones. Each batch was a little different. Some were a little heavier or a little lighter. Some were unbalanced. The last batch was yellow. "Knuckleballs thrown with out of round baseballs should have very difficult mathematics," Gates had predicted. "I don't know how long it will take them to figure it out, or if they will ever figure it out, but while they are trying, there should be a large number of transmissions for us to triangulate and decipher."

Finally, with preparations all in place and technicians standing by, Gates and Norton went up to their command center to wait for game time.

The command center was built into the luxury suite next to George

Steinbrenner's skybox. Behind one-way glass, Gates and his team could look out on the field without being observed. Communication equipment connected all the task force leaders. Several computer stations were lined up against the back wall, all manned by Microsoft engineers. A special guest in the booth was Jamail Hawthorne, a 16-year-old black kid from the projects of the South Bronx. Jamail was the reigning computer game world champion. Not knowing exactly what he was up against, Gates hoped to be prepared for every eventuality.

Tired and sleep deprived, but energized by the challenge ahead, Gates sat down in his command chair elevated in the front of the box. From there, his view of the action in the box and on the field was unobstructed. Peter Norton sat in a smaller version of the chair to Gates' right. To a certain extent, this was Gates' dream come true. He had always been a secret admirer of Star Trek. When he designed the command center, he had the bridge of the Starship Enterprise in mind. In all his years behind the scenes at Microsoft, there had never been this kind of drama. For the next few hours, he would fulfill his lifelong ambition of being Captain Kirk. East Timor would be his personal Klingons.

Meanwhile, Tim Wakefield, forty-two years old and graying, with a sore arm and an arthritic back, picked up one of the special baseballs and released the first pitch.

CHAPTER 19

"Strike Three!"

Snemelc C. went down on three pitches as A. and B. before him. The major leaguers had caught a break with the weather. It was a hot, dry day. Wakefield's knucklers were dancing so much that the batters weren't coming close to contact. Pudge Rodriguez was having an equally hard time catching them. Every third or fourth ball sailed to the backstop. Snemelc stood at the plate after whiffing and pounded his bat in disgust. The all-stars invigorated with new hope ran in from the field. The small crowd cheered. After nine innings of humiliation, they finally had something to cheer about.

In the command post, Peter Norton monitored his instruments. He looked up at Bill Gates. "We're detecting a flurry of transmissions from several sources. All of the information seems to be doubly encrypted. We are going to need a lot more data to break this code. Hopefully, once we do, they won't switch to a backup."

Jamail Hawthorne put down his game boy and walked over. "I wouldn't count on it," he said. "These boys are familiar with game theory, and every game has multiple levels. Hopefully, they won't figure out that we're on to them, or they will switch protocols."

"Where did you come up with that?" Norton asked.

"Grand Theft Auto," Jamail replied.

"I wouldn't think they could sense our instruments," Norton said, "even though I wouldn't put anything past them. It looks to me that their strategy is to bombard us with so many transmissions, that we can't identify the live one."

"Can you?" Gates asked.

"I don't know," Norton replied. "This is a huge undertaking. Eventually, we can break any code. Right now, time isn't on our side."

Back on the field, the all-stars were having little success against Snemelc L. Ichiro, Jeter and A-Rod struck out back to back. The radar gun had L. at 117 miles an hour. Only Ichiro was even able to foul off a few pitches. Tommy Lasorda watched quietly from the dugout. There was nothing he could do or say. Tommy hated the helpless feeling. He hated even more the way L. ridiculed the game after every pitch, going to the rosin bag, tugging on the chain around his neck and smoothing out the rubber. Everyone who was ever around Tommy knew him as a passionate, but respectful man. Few knew that Tommy had a dark side. At that moment, he was fantasizing about charging the mound with a bat and beating L. senseless, and then taking on Snemelcs A. thru K.

When the second inning started, the umpires were instructed to change balls after every foul so that different unbalanced balls would present different mathematical challenges. Inning by inning, Wakefield retired the side. One by one, Peter Norton scanned all transmissions and forwarded them to his lab. By the sixth inning, the score was still zero to zero, but Gates was beginning to worry. In each successive frame, the Snemelcs were making more and better contact. In the fifth inning, they put two balls in play and even managed one hit. Peter Norton had determined that he could not break the code in time to influence game two.

In the home half of the seventh, with the game still scoreless, the all-stars went on the offensive. Bob Sheppard, the long time PA announcer at the stadium, announced a pinch hitter. "May I have your attention please? Batting next for the Major Leaguers, please welcome Willie Mays." The crowd went silent. What the heck was going on? "This must be some mistake," John Sterling commented from the broadcast booth. "Willie is in his seventies and almost blind. He's facing one hundred plus mile an hour heaters. He could get killed out there." But there he was, walking slowly to the plate wearing his old number twenty-four.

Snemelc L. stared in at the batter for a few extra seconds as if something didn't compute. He looked confused, but then suddenly, he smiled. He wound up and lobbed the ball right over the center of the plate at about seventy miles an hour. Mays swung and drove one into the gap. "What the hell!" shouted Sterling, as Mays headed around first. Then, mysteriously, the center fielder muffed the ball on purpose, pretending to miss the carom of the wall. He followed with a terrible throw that missed the cutoff man. Mays limped around the bases at a snail's pace and scored the game's first run. The crowd initially didn't know how to react but then started screaming. Not only had the home team scored, but it was scored by the 'Say Hey' kid, still a big favorite in New York.

In the command post, Gates jumped out of his seat. He had guessed right. The East Timorean players had watched every inning of recorded baseball. They had been taught to mimic all of the game's conventions. You always let the Old-Timers win.

Jamail ran over to Norton. "Jam all frequencies now!" he screamed. "We need another run." Sure enough, the sequence was repeated with

Yogi Berra and Stan Musial. While Glickman and Bostwick were coughing up their beer, the Snemelcs were laughing, smiling, and patting the runners as they went around the bases. Lasorda was about to send Carl Yastrzemski to the plate were he heard Gates on his headset. "They have gone to another frequency which we can't detect. Go to step two. Repeat, go to step two."

Lasorda kept his other pinch hitters on the bench. After the next three batters struck out, the seventh inning was over. The all-stars were up by three.

In the top of the eighth, the East Timor started to hit Wakefield. Snemelc E. lined out to first, but F. hit the next knuckler into the bullpen for a homer. Gates had seen enough. He hit a button on his command consul and talked to the equipment room. "Time for the yellow balls," he ordered. Bob Sheppard explained over the PA system that the special yellow balls would be put in play for one out each. They would then be sent to hospitals around the world. Gates had a theory that the reflective metallic paint that was dotted on the balls' surface would confuse the batters. The all-stars needed only five more outs. As they had planned, Lasorda signaled to Pudge to have Wakefield abandon the knuckler and throw his pathetic batting practice fastballs. It worked. Snemelc G. swung late and hit a grounder to Reyes at second for an easy out, but H. connected and hit a bullet line drive over Jones' head in center. H. was motoring around the bases at sprinter's speed. When he rounded third and headed for the plate, Gates hit a button on his control board. All of a sudden, Kate Smith came over the loudspeaker singing God Bless America and an American flag appeared on the video scoreboard. Jamail had thought of this one. Half way between third and home, H. stopped, turned to the flag, stood at attention and took off his helmet. A-Rod took the relay from Reyes and tagged him out. Another bullet dodged. On to the bottom of the eighth.

In the command center, the team had mixed feelings. Their tricks were working, but they were burning their lifelines too quickly. They had hoped that the knuckleball would have bought them more innings before East Timor figured it out. They had wanted to save God Bless America for game three, but they knew that if they lost today, the series would be over.

In the home half, Pujols managed to hit a soft grounder through the middle for a single, but Guerrero, Jones and Pudge left him stranded. The crowd took a deep breath and waited for the ninth.

Chapter 20

The top of the ninth All-stars 3, East Timor 1

As Snemelc I. came to the plate, Glickman and Bostwick looked down from their box. They had started to spend some of their $500,000,000, and now things weren't going according to plan. The 'party girls' in the box with them were doing everything in their power to earn their keep, groping, hugging and just being seen, but their bosses were more interested in the action on the field.

In the command center, Billy Gates was wondering out loud if Wakefield had another inning in his 42-year-old arm, or if it was time to go to the bullpen. He buzzed Lasorda in the dugout. Before Tommy responded, Jamail came up to the bridge. "Get his ass off the mound," Jamail advised. "They've got his number." Lasorda and Gates disagreed. Logic implied that since they had no sure stopper in the bullpen, they would stick with the devil they had rather than the one they might get. They should have listened to Jamail. Knuckler or no knuckler, unbalanced yellow ball or not, Snemelc I. was ready. He hit the first pitch into the same seat that all the homers hit in game one. The score was three to two.

Just when things were beginning to look grim, Peter Norton jumped up from his chair and screamed, "We've found the feed. We've found the feed. They are transmitting from the hot dog stand in the right field bleachers. The signal is routing through a low orbiting satellite. I think I can block them for about ten minutes while they reroute. Do you want me to blast them?"

"Not yet," Gates commanded, and just as he had observed Captain Kirk so many times, he said, "Block them on my signal." He buzzed Lasorda, "Tommy, time to go to the bull pen."

As Lasorda walked to the mound, John Sterling spoke into the radio mike, "The bottom of the ninth, a one run game, $1,000,000,000 on the line. You know what that means. It's Mariano time." He looked at Susan Waldman, his color man. "Mariano Rivera is the greatest pressure closer of all time. Does he have another big game in his arm?"

Lasorda went out to the mound and took the ball from Wakefield. The old pitcher got a standing ovation from the crowd as he walked off the field. The stands were full. As the game had progressed, many of the ticket holders had decided to come back to the park.

Lasorda signaled to the pen. Mariano took off his warm up jacket and headed to the gate. Sterling started to say "here he comes," but wait, it wasn't Mariano. A skinny kid that looked all of twelve years old was walking to the infield. "Now pitching," Bob Sheppard announced, "in his major league debut, Timmy Taylor." The crowd stopped cheering. Again, there was dead silence.

"Should I jam them now?" Norton asked.

"Not yet," Gates replied. "That won't give us enough time. They do their adjustments between batters. We will jam them after the first out." He looked up in the air, "That is if there is a first out."

Timmy took the ball, and as he had been instructed, he didn't take any warm up throws for Snemelc A. to measure. Everyone was on the edge of their seats, everyone, that is except for Jamail Hawthorne.

"They could have watched every pitch in recorded time," he said, "but they ain't never seen anything like this." So confident was he that he pulled a Game Boy out of his pocket and started playing Super Mario Three.

Timmy Taylor took the ball and wound up. He grunted and flung the ball towards the plate. Snemelc A. took a mighty swing and hit an easy chopper to short. Jeter gobbled it up and went to first, one away.

"Now," commanded Gates. Norton hit the red button on his console. A humming noise emanated from the booth. "We've got about 10 minutes," Norton exclaimed.

Snemelc B. stepped up to the plate. Taylor looked in for the sign. He shook off Rodriguez. "What the fuck is he doing?" Gates gasped, very much out of character for a man who hated profanity. "We only have eight minutes left."

"Hell, Mr. Gates," Jamail answered, "every kid in the world wants to be on the mound at the stadium in the bottom of the ninth and shake off a sign from his catcher. Give the kid a break."

On the field, Snemelc B. stepped out of the batters box and adjusted his glasses. With a puzzled look on his face, he stepped back in. Taylor delivered. B. swung and hit a lazy floater to Pujols at first. There were two away, one out from game three. Gates looked at his watch, four minutes to go. Then, Snemelc L., the acting manager, came out of the dugout and ambled slowly towards the home plate umpire. "Shit!" Gates said under his breath. "He is on to us. He's stalling for time. How much longer can you jam them?" he looked to Norton.

"It looks like they are diverting their signal off another satellite as we speak," Norton replied.

Gates was frantic. He looked at Jamail who was playing his Game

Boy peacefully, oblivious to the high drama. "Where are we now?" he asked the kid.

Jamail didn't look up. "Where we are now is we are screwed," he replied. He paused for a moment enjoying his position of making the richest man in the world sweat, "unless of course, the power went out in the whole stadium."

Gates lunged for his mike and hailed the control room. "Kill the power!" he yelled.

In the stadium control room, Jake Puck, the seventyish head grounds keeper put down his baloney sandwich. "What was that you said, Mr. Gates?"

Gates screamed into the mike at the top of his voice. "Kill the fucking power, and kill it now!" Puck took another bite of his lunch. Then, he walked over to the electric panel and pulled the master switch.

Fortunately, it was still light out, and the game continued. Snemelc L. went back to the dugout. Snemelc C. stepped up to the plate. Taylor wound and delivered. Apparently, East Timor had made a partial transmission before the power went out. C. swung and hit a high fly towards the wall in the deepest part of center field. Tori Hunter, possibly the best defensive center fielder in baseball history, had gone into the game in the bottom of the eighth. He galloped toward the warning track. When he reached the wall, he jumped. His glove hand extended into the stands. The crowd gasped in silence and then screamed. Hunter had made the catch. He brought the ball back for the third out. The game was over. The all-stars had won three to two. On to game three.

In the command post, the team jumped up and down for a few seconds and then, composed themselves. There was no time to celebrate. They needed to start their preparations for the series finale.

The next day, in the paper, the box score read, winning pitcher, Tim Wakefield, save, Tim Taylor, save number one, one inning pitched.

Chapter 21

When the post game press conference got underway, Jim Grey was sitting in the first row. He couldn't wait to ask the long list of questions he had prepared. Up until now, he had been the forgotten member of the team. If the stars had lost game two, he would not have been able to showcase his talents. On the podium, there were several chairs set up behind a long table with a microphone in front of each chair. Tommy Lasorda and Garden Bostwick sat down next to each other. To Lasorda's right sat Tim Wakefield and Tori Hunter, the stars of the game. Next to Guffy sat Snemelcs A. and E. for no apparent reason. While the Major League stars wore handsome warm-ups, the East Timoreans wore their same sickening lime green. Following the normal format, Bostwick and Lasorda would make opening comments before opening the floor to a Q and A.

Guffy went first. He made some very generic comments congratulating the stars on their victory. He said how much he was looking forward to game three. Then, his tone changed. He said he was sorry to see the game degenerate into a sideshow of old-timers and cheap tricks. He concluded by saying that he hoped the series finale would be a true test of classic baseball.

Not unexpectedly, Tommy Lasorda was less diplomatic. "Nothing would make me happier than classic baseball," Tommy exclaimed.

"Then, we could kick all of the Snemelcs in the ass and give them a one way ticket back to the crap hole that they came from." He paused for a second, "and if you want to know what I really think about these rejects from clown school..." Before he could complete his sentence, Brian Cashman took the mike and finished, "What Tommy means to say is that everyone in the baseball world is excited to see what a fine team East Timor has fielded. The game itself is the greatest beneficiary of this tournament that spreads our national pastime to all the corners of the earth."

While Brian was talking, Snemelcs A. and E. started scratching their arms and face in an animated manner. The pressroom focused on their actions. No one understood what was happening. Finally, Cashman spotted Jamail in the corner of the room with a dog whistle in his mouth and a big smile on his face. Cashman gave him the finger across the throat sign. With a big grin, Jamail put the whistle in his pocket, and the conference continued.

Jim Grey stood up for the first question. He addressed Snemelc A. "We understand that East Timor has a tradition of active nightlife. What does your soul tell you when you dance?" Grey had stayed up all night coming up with that one. "You little bastard," he thought to himself, "every time you look at me, you will wonder where that question came from. Let's see if you can get that out of your mind when you need to concentrate on game three."

Before A. could answer, Guffy Bostwick grabbed his mike, "My players will answer questions on the game only."

Grey followed up, "I see, Mr. Bostwick. This was supposed to be an open Q and A. Is there something you are trying to hide? Perhaps the pressure of a one billion dollar bet is beginning to get under your skin?

Is there anything to the rumor that your sponsors are backing off, or that they can't come up with the money?"

"You know that our money is in escrow with the United Bank of Switzerland. Next question."

Grey was unrelenting. This was his chance to show the world that he had superior investigative skills than the correspondents from Sixty Minutes and Dateline. "Is there any truth to the rumor that you are communicating to your players on the field with electronic devices? That is against baseball rules you know."

"Really sir," Guffy replied. "we will win the game because East Timor has superior players." He took a quick peek at Tommy Lasorda. "I trust tomorrow we can play real baseball, and the Major League all-stars won't hide behind seventy year old has-beens."

Tommy Lasorda started to get up out of his seat, but Brian Cashman restrained him again. For another half an hour, the cadre of carefully picked reporters fired question after question designed to disrupt Team East Timor's composure.

While the press conference was going on, Billy Gates had assembled the other members of the team in the Yankee boardroom. He spoke to each one of his 'commandos' assigning their tasks. He turned to Jennifer. "Miss Stone, we need to get our hands on a pair of the East Timor eyeglasses. K. is pitching tomorrow. We need his. Replace them with these. They look identical, and if you can make the switch, they won't suspect anything."

"I'm on it boss," Jennifer declared as she got up and left the room.

"Peter, if we get the glasses, we need to figure out how to send disinformation, how to tell them to throw fat ones right over the center of the plate. Jamming isn't good enough. With a night to prepare, they will have anticipated jamming. I am sure that's why Glickman isn't at the press conference. We will have to be able to override their signals."

"Mr. Singh," Gates purposely called him Mr. instead of professor as the scientist preferred, "you will be the perfect person to create a diversion, some grand spectacle or whatever, if we need to delay the game and buy some time, maybe some ceremony to recognize an important event in East Timor's history."

As much as Singh was pouting over being upstaged by Gates, he was still pleased to be delegated such an important task. "My people will make all the arrangements," he said. He pulled an aerosol out of his pocket and sprayed some breath mint into his mouth. "Only the stone of destiny can roll up hill," he expounded. As he arose, his assistants gathered up his computers and papers and followed him out.

Gates turned his attention to the stadium's head grounds keeper who had been asked to join the meeting. "Mr. Puck, tonight, I want you to kick everyone out of the stadium, and I mean everyone. When it is empty and totally dark, I want you to move the rubber back two inches. Can you do it without being noticed?"

"Yes sir, Mr. Gates. I will attend to that personally." Jake headed out the door.

"That should do it, gentlemen," Gates concluded. The only people left in the room with him were Giuliani, Steinbrenner and Jamail Hawthorne. They were about to leave when the elevator door sprung open. Tommy Lasorda entered having just finished the press conference. He brought a guest with him, a big, tall Texan wearing a cowboy hat. His guest needed no introduction in that room as he was one of the greatest pitchers of all time. Standing next to Tommy was the one and only Roger Clemens. "Sorry I missed the meeting boys," Lasorda said, "but I wanted to introduce you to tomorrow's starting pitcher."

CHAPTER 22

After a Hall of Fame career, Roger Clemens was having a tough time walking away from the game. He had retired three times only to return each of the following seasons. He had hung up his spikes for good last year. Still, he worked out continuously, keeping himself in top shape. Like the prizefighter that thinks he has one more comeback in him, the Rocket could never put the spotlight out of his mind. He was the most feared pitcher in his era and the fiercest competitor. If Al Qaeda invaded Manhattan, he was the man to stand behind. Nevertheless, he had been out of baseball for over a year, and George Steinbrenner had reservations. He asked Tommy Lasorda. "This is the biggest game ever played. Do we want to come at them with another knuckleballer?"

"There isn't another knuckleballer," Tommy replied.

"Besides," Gates chipped in, "they've got the knuckleball figured out."

The Boss had never forgiven Clemens for defecting from the Yankees to Houston a couple of seasons ago, but now with the fate of the free world hanging in balance, he agreed that there was no one else to put on the mound. "Do you have one victory left in that big right arm?" he asked.

"I can do it skip," Clemens replied. "In fact, I am meeting with

Pudge over at Shea Stadium in an hour to warm up with the rubber pulled back a few inches."

Clemens had that look in his eye. It was the look of strength and defiance that both Gates and Steinbrenner recognized. It was a look that said, "Don't fuck with me. Just get out of the way." Since this was probably the last time he would ever pitch, pitch counts, his elbow, his shoulder, nothing mattered. He could leave it all on the field.

"Why do you want to do this, Roger?" Giuliani asked. "What's in it for you?"

"Everyone wants to go out in style," he replied. "This exit is one that I could never have dreamed of. Besides, I owe it to the game." He gathered his thoughts for a minute. "Another thing, I don't like the way those pricks made fun of my name. They better stay away from the inside of the plate."

"My thoughts exactly," Tommy added.

The meeting ended. Roger went to loosen up with Pudge. Tommy and Giuliani went to get a little sleep. Billy Gates and Peter Norton ordered a pot of coffee and headed downstairs for a long night in the computer center. As they left the room, Jamail tagged behind like a lap dog, a backpack over his shoulder and his head immersed in a brand new portable X Box that Gates had given him as a gift.

Chapter 23

It took Jennifer three attempts to switch Snemelc K.'s glasses. When East Timor's bus arrived at their hotel, she was waiting in full groupie attire. If she could just get close enough to K., she would ask for his autograph, bump into him, knock his glasses to the ground and make the switch. Unfortunately, try as she might, she couldn't muscle her way through the crowd of reporters. She got close, but just as she was honing in for the kill, a sleazy looking reporter from the National Enquirer shoved her out of the way and snapped a picture. After getting his shot, he turned to Jennifer apologetically. "Hey missy," he said in a Cockney accent, "sorry about that. Can I buy you a pint at the hotel bar?"

Jennifer feigned interest as she sidled up next to him, "Oh, let me see." Then, she gave him a violent knee to the groin, followed by smacking him upside the face with her purse sending him down to the pavement. "I think not. Maybe some other time."

Her next sortie was in the dining room that East Timor had reserved for their team meal. A few bucks in the right hands, and she had a job serving dinner. True to form, she picked out a waitress uniform a couple of sizes too small. Again, she awaited an opportunity to make a move. She planned to spill some hot soup on K. That would give her the chance to make the switch under the guise of cleaning his glasses. At the last second, she was thwarted again. This time, it was a big, pimple faced teenager, who wanted to make time with her by offering to carry her tray of soup. He wouldn't take no for an answer. She had to abort for fear of making a scene. Back in the kitchen, the gallant lad cornered Jennifer and was about to ask her out, when suddenly, she grabbed him by the back of the neck and gave him a big, wet kiss. His face went beet red. Then, she slipped him the room key that she had lifted from the big, fat, fiftyish lady cook.

Her mission was accomplished on the third try. Billy Gates had given her a big wad of bills, and she spread them around liberally. She persuaded a maid to lend her uniform and go home early. After the team's lights were out, Jennifer slipped into K.'s room. He and two teammates were laying under the covers in a king sized bed. "How cute," she observed. All of them were in an identical position with their thumbs in their mouths. K.'s glasses were in plain sight on the dresser. "So easy," the detective thought as she made the switch. Just then, she heard a key in the door. With nowhere to hide, she dove into bed with the three Snemelcs and hid under the covers. The door opened. Garden Bostwick took a quick look to make sure his players were accounted for, then closed the door and left. Jennifer lay still for a moment and then rolled out of the bed. As she did, one of the Snemelcs turned over and looked at her. The other two continued snoring undisturbed. Thinking quickly, Jennifer kissed him on the forehead and whispered into his ear to go back to sleep. Like a charm, he rolled back to his position and in a minute was snoring again. When she was sure the coast was clear, she slipped out of the hotel, hopped behind the wheel of her Jag and sped back to the stadium.

A little after midnight, she rushed into the computer room with a big smile on her face. “I’ve got a little gift for you, Billy,” she exclaimed in her sweetest tone. Gates took the glasses and handed them to an assistant who took off running to the lab set up in the adjoining room.

“Good job, Jennifer,” Gates was pleased. “How did you do them?”

“Oh, nothing special, but I did find out one interesting thing.”

“What was that, Jennifer?” Gates asked always looking for more usable data.

“Well,” Jennifer replied, “I got to see K. up close and personal, and he really is major league in more ways than one.”

Gates decided not to ask for further clarification.

Jennifer started to leave thinking her task was completed, but a bleary-eyed Peter Norton stopped her. “Jennifer,” he said, “the glasses are invaluable. We will be running diagnostics all night, but you can’t go yet. We will be making some special modifications and then…,” he paused, “we will need your special talents to switch them back.”

Chapter 24

Working nonstop, Peter Norton's crew finished their modifications on K.'s glasses at 1:15 P.M., one hour before game time. Making the second switch turned out to be easy. As East Timor was dressing for the game, the door to their locker room flew open. A slew of federal agents rushed in leading teams of dogs and carrying a variety of instruments. "Nothing to worry about," the squad commander announced. "Some crank called in a bomb scare. The threat isn't credible, but we will give the room the once over just to be on the safe side. If everyone would move away from their lockers for just a moment, we will be out of here in no time."

The squad commander was in fact a federal agent, but the rest of the crew was comprised of actors that Tom Cruise and Jennifer had recruited. In fact, Cruise himself, disguised with a fake beard and mustache was part of the team. He looked under the chairs and benches, waiving a Palm Pilot that was programmed to beep every few seconds. Jennifer Stone, wearing a blond wig and heavy makeup pretended to inspect the lockers. Arriving at K.'s locker, she made the switch without any notice. Jennifer winked at the commander who proclaimed the search was complete and ordered the agents to pull out. The team, however, was having too much fun to leave right away. After about five more minutes of careful dusting and sniffing, they followed Tom

Cruise out of the clubhouse, down the hall and around the corner to their dressing rooms. There, they changed into the next set of costumes. There was one more important scene to play.

Outside the stadium, crowds were gathering. Tickets that were being given away after game one, were now selling for fifteen hundred bucks apiece. The usual Big Apple celebrities were arriving at this 'must be seen at event'. Television screens were being set up in the stadium plaza for the overflow. Closed circuit feeds were wired to paying gates at Madison Square Garden, the Nassau Coliseum and to Major League ballparks around the country. So great was the national interest, that the finals of American Idol, scheduled for the same evening, were postponed to another date.

With game time approaching, players, management and technicians from both teams were making final preparations. In the clubhouse, Tommy Lasorda was letting it all hang out. "Remember boys, this is the Real World Series. If you lose this game, you will regret it till the day you die." He paused for a second. When he continued, his voice was breaking with emotion, "Give it your best, gentlemen. There might be some youngster in the stands watching you for the first time."

In the command center, Peter Norton was busy checking and rechecking his equipment. He paced up and down behind a line of technicians sitting at desks covered with instruments and computer screens. Billy Gates was up on the bridge contacting all of his tactical support groups. In their dressing room, the actors, under the direction of Tom Cruise, were hurriedly changing from their bomb squad outfits into New York City Police uniforms.

As television sets and radios from Cuba to Tokyo tuned into the game, John Sterling, the voice of the Yankees, stepped up to his microphone. Roger Clemens finished his warm up tosses and as only he could do, glared into East Timor's dugout. Snemelc A. Regor stepped into the batters box and knocked the dirt off his spikes with his bat. Tommy Lasorda tugged on the cross hanging from the chain around his neck. The home plate umpire adjusted his mask. "Play ball," he commanded.

CHAPTER 25

Against a deafening roar, the Rocket wound up and let fly. The pitch, a fastball in the high nineties, knocked Snemelc A. to the ground. The game was on. The umpires immediately warned each bench about throwing at batters, but the first pitch was no surprise. Everyone expected that from Roger. The message was simple. "I don't appreciate you clowns making fun of my name and the game," and, "keep your heads up because I mean business."

The next pitch was another fastball off the inside of the plate. Snemelc A. hit a hard line drive foul by a couple of inches. The third pitch was Clemens' out pitch, a nasty splitter dropping down out of the strike zone. A. swung and topped the ball, hitting an easy grounder to Jeter at short. Jeter had to rush his throw as all the Snemelcs were fast runners, but managed to get the out. In the dugout, Tommy Lasorda smiled. In this, the biggest game ever, Roger Clemens had his best stuff. Rested and motivated, he would hopefully be able to go long into the game. In the command center, Billy Gates wiped his brow. Pulling the first pitch and topping the second meant that East Timor was swinging early and high. They hadn't figured out that with the rubber two inches back, the mathematics of the pitches were altered. He hoped that it would take several innings for them to catch on. Meanwhile, Peter Norton and his team were monitoring all of East Timor's transmissions through the duplicate eyeglasses that had been procured courtesy of Jennifer Stone. They were preparing logistics for the final assault.

In the owner's box, Brian Cashman was doing his best to keep George Steinbrenner calm. The Boss was chewing what little fingernails that he had left. He continued to look back and forth from the action on the field to the box seats behind the Yankee dugout. In those seats sat Pierre Stahl, a representative of the United Bank of Switzerland. Stahl was surrounded by lawyers and bodyguards. The United Bank, or UBS as it was referred to, had been designated special escrow agent for the big wager. In a briefcase handcuffed to his wrist were signed bank agreements authorizing the transfer of $500,000,000 as well as a quitclaim deed to the New York Yankees. In addition, the briefcase contained signed paperwork to mortgage Steinbrenner's shipping company, his commercial real estate, his home and all his other property as collateral for his payment.

Snemelc B. settled into the batters box, adjusted his batting gloves, spit in the dirt and went through all the motions lampooning major leaguers. Clemens wound up and delivered. With his adrenalin pumping, his fastball hit the gun at ninety-eight miles per hour, two miles an hour faster than the first. B. swung and got out in front of it. He hit a fly ball down the left field line. Vlad Guerrero sprinted towards the corner. Because Yankee Stadium was originally built on real estate too small for a normal ballpark, there was little room in foul territory in the outfield. The hard concrete wall made it dangerous for fielders chasing balls down the line. Guerrero had one of the best arms in baseball but was never known for his fielding prowess. Running at full speed, he made a leaping one-handed catch before crashing into the concrete wall. Hitting the ground in a limp pile, he managed to hold on to the ball. As the crowd cheered, the rest of the team had that special feeling in the pit of their stomach that they were part of something special. In the dugout, Tommy Lasorda wiped a tear from his eye. He felt akin to an army lieutenant sending a young GI to storm a bunker, knowing that he might be sending the kid to his death. His players were putting it all on the line for him.

Over the years, as computers became more and more powerful, they replaced human beings in numerous and sophisticated tasks. With the ability to make thousands of calculations per second, and the ability to analyze systems, they became superior in countless new ways. In spite of that, the best human chess and poker players had always been able to beat the most powerful computers. The moral of the story is that the human brain and the human spirit have that intangible quality that allowed the human race to adapt and survive over thousands of years. No computer had ever been built with that same ability. Today, game three would be another test of human resolve against the most powerful of all technologies. All of a sudden, Tommy Lasorda and his all-stars felt that they had a chance.

With every pitch, Clemens was getting faster, and his balls were breaking more sharply. He was getting to the zone that only few people ever achieve in their lifetime. He was starting to feel invincible. Snemelc C. stepped into the box. He hit the first fastball foul. The second popped foul into the seats. The third pitch, another splitter dropped like a rock. C. swung and missed; strike three. Clemens pounded his fist and walked off the mound glaring at C. C. said something. Clemens started walking towards him before Jeter got between and led his pitcher back to the dugout. The message was clear.

This was war, and the Rocket didn't plan to lose.

Ichiro led off for the stars in the bottom of the first. K's first offering, a slider, which at normal pitching distance would have been an unhittable strike, broke half an inch out of the zone. All of his pitches were close, but he ended up issuing a walk. In the command post, Tankai Lu was monitoring the transmissions. "They are going through the math," he announced. "It is just a matter of time till they make the adjustments. We better score and score quickly."

At the same time, a second assistant was triangulating the origin of the transmissions. "We have it narrowed down to a three block radius in the South Bronx." He handed a computer generated map to Gates.

Gates picked up his mike and spoke to his 'DEA' team headed by Giuliani, Stone and Cruise. "Get the team to the Bronx staging ground," he ordered. "We will have the exact location shortly."

Meanwhile, Derek Jeter stepped up to the plate and looked down at his third base coach for the signs being relayed from the dugout.

Chapter 26

K.'s first two pitches to Jeter were fastballs out of the zone, but each one missed by less than the one before. In the command center, Tankai had translated East Timor's code. In perfect English, he informed Gates that he believed they were compensating for what they thought was some type of atmospheric deviation, maybe barometric pressure, but they were still unaware that the pitching distance had been altered. "That," he exclaimed, "still gives us a workable advantage."

The next two pitches were strikes, one hundred and ten mile an hour fastballs, unhittable to a normal human being. Fortunately for the all-stars, a normal human being wasn't at the plate. After K.'s next offering, a seventy mile an hour change broke low, Jeter fouled off the next twelve pitches. In doing so, he broke four bats. The thirteenth pitch could have been called a ball or a strike, but Charlie Rutherford, the home plate ump, called it a ball putting Jeter on first and moving Ichiro to second.

A word about the umpires, to their credit, they had made every call with integrity and without bias. They knew that if East Timor won, their careers could be over and their livelihoods ruined. Nevertheless, they were professionals, and their respect for the game won over their dislike for the lime green ball club.

Alex Rodriguez stepped up to the plate and took a couple of practice swings. Acknowledged as the best all-around player in the world before the Snemelcs came onto the scene, he was coming off a tough season in the Bronx. Last year, he had made an unusual amount of errors in the field and struck out too often with runners on base. By the end of the season, every mistake he made was followed by jeers from Yankee fans in the stands. In the command center, Jamail whispered something into Gates' ear. Gates relayed the message to Lasorda in the dugout, and then the unthinkable happened. A-Rod squared and laid down a perfect sacrifice bunt. East Timor was caught off guard. An MVP bunting with runners at first and second and no outs in the first inning wasn't supposed to happen. The third baseman threw Alex out at first, but Ichiro and Jeter advanced to second and third.

"How did you know that would work?" an impressed Bill Gates asked Jamail.

"Simple," Jamail responded as he continued to play Madden football on his X box. "You said that East Timor had loaded every play in baseball history into their database. That was the first time in his career that A-Rod has ever bunted."

As David Ortiz approached the plate, every one of the fans in the stadium was standing. Unfortunately, the East Timor programmers had made some adjustments. Ortiz struck out on three pitches. In the control center, a sweaty and nervous Gates was afraid that they had lost their big advantage. "Not so," said Jamail, who was now standing by his side. "Time to use your first power pill. This will need perfect execution and timing. Allow me." With that, he radioed for Tommy Lasorda to put on the steal sign.

On the field, Ichiro and Jeter were so surprised that they brushed their forearm, the baseball convention asking the manager to repeat the signs. No one ever stole home in this era. The steal sign was flashed again. K. wound up, and Ichiro broke for home. Just before K. released the ball, Jamail pushed the blue button on the control consol, hitting K. with 200,000 bytes of data. K. jerked, and the ball sailed wildly over his catcher's head. Ichiro, breaking for the plate, scored easily. "That will only work once," Jamail exclaimed with a big cheesy grin on his face.

In the dugout, the expression on Roger Clemens' face went from resolute to demonic. There is an urban myth in baseball, told to all rookies in their first year, that the great pitchers when they have their best stuff need only one run to win big games. When a Sandy Koufax or a Nolan Ryan had it going, the first run their team scored unleashed a demon that thinks itself invulnerable. Clemens was holding his favorite metal cup filled with Gatorade. Without thinking, his left hand crushed the cup and threw it clanking to the dugout floor as if it was thin paper. As his face turned to a light shade of purple, his teammates sitting near got up and left him alone at the end of the bench. Not only did they want to give him some space, but actually, in his present state, Roger scared them to death. When the next batter, Albert Pujols, struck out, the stars took the field for the second inning leading one to nothing.

In the command center, Peter Norton had some bad news. East Timor had a backup plan with fresh frequencies. Norton was impressed. The opposition had been prepared for this contingency. There would be no way decipher new codes in time. His role in the contest might be over.

Billy Gates was distraught when Norton gave him the news. Just when victory seemed within their grasp, East Timor had outsmarted them again. By now, the tycoon hadn't slept five hours in the last six days, and he was starting to get rummy. With this last wrinkle thrown at him by the East Timor technicians, he realized that he was at the end of his rope. He looked around the room ponderously while he thought through his last, big decision, and then he made an unexpected announcement. "It is time," he said, "for Jamail to assume the bridge." With that, the richest man in the world stepped down from his chair, and the young black teen from the projects assumed control. In later years, as the Gates legend grew, this was hailed as one of his greatest moments. He realized that the field of conflict had advanced from technology to gaming theory. It was time to cede to the reigning champion.

On the field, Clemens was taking it to a new level. Pudge Rodriguez stopped giving him signs. Roger would get the ball, rear back and throw. There was nothing in the East Timor database for a future Hall of Famer letting it all hang out while pitching his last game. With the help of some great fielding, Clemens retired Snemelcs D. through F. Clemens was in that mythical zone. If you had been able to get close enough to ask him a question, he probably couldn't have told you his birth date or his mother's maiden name.

The next five innings were a classic pitching duel. Not one all-star reached base. In every inning, East Timor was getting better swings and more base runners, but Roger would not break. In the top of the seventh, East Timor loaded the bases with two outs on a single and two walks. It looked like the Rocket was running out of gas. Lasorda called time and headed out to the mound. Pudge and the other infielders gathered around their star pitcher expecting to have a discussion and offer their encouragement. Lasorda walked right past them and got right into the Rocket's face. His words were short and succinct. "Roger," he said irritably, "get the fucking ball over the plate!" A tired

Clemens thought for a second and his jaw clenched. “OK skip,” he replied, “now get the fuck off my mound.”

Clemens first two offerings to H. were the fastest pitches he had thrown in his life. H. watched them go by for called strikes. Clemens knew that with the bases loaded a hit could spell big trouble. He glared in at Pudge, wound up and threw. H. took a vicious cut and cork screwed into the dirt. Strike three. As Pudge rolled the ball back to the mound, he noticed that it was covered with bloody fingerprints.

Chapter 27

The bottom of the seventh started with a bad sign of things to come. When Snemelc K. walked out to the mound, he looked right into the dugout and grinned. He rearranged some dirt before he toed the rubber effectively compensating for the two-inch difference. He struck out Andruw Jones, Pudge Rodriguez and Jose Reyes on nine pitches. The batters were over-matched. They did not come close to making contact. In fact, they looked more like school kids waving butterfly nets, than Major League hitters. K. tipped his cap in Lasorda's direction as he walked off the field. It was a good thing that there were several security guards in the dugout. Tommy started onto the field with a bat in his hand. David Ortiz, one of the game's gentlemen, was right behind him. He had a bat in each hand. New York's finest brought them back to the dugout without incident. Ichiro channeled his anger against the Gatorade container. With a well-placed kick, plastic and Gatorade flew in all directions. He made some comments in Japanese that no one understood. Yoshi, his interpreter, started blushing. "One thing for certain," Tommy thought to himself as the security guards led him back to his seat, " the boys don't need a pep talk."

In the command center, the team had worried looks on their faces. Now that East Timor had figured out the pitching distance, a tired Roger Clemens would be a dead duck. Billy Gates slumped in his chair.

Fatigue was getting the best of him. Rising up like an old prizefighter answering the last bell, he walked to Jamail at the bridge and grabbed the headset. He contacted Giuliani. “Rudy,” he said, “we need to disable their command and control. Time is becoming critical. How close are you?”

“We’ve got the location narrowed down to one last block,” the former mayor answered, “but this is tough terrain. We have one hundred cops knocking on doors. We should find them within the hour.”

“Roger that,” Gates replied. Then, making an attempt at a baseball metaphor, “We are getting down to our last out.”

The only one in the command center that didn’t seem worried was Jamail Hawthorne. His placid expression had given way to steely resolve. He put down his X Box and concentrated on the control panel. Up until now, this had been kids stuff. It was time to get serious. Jamail remembered *Revenge of the Ninja*, the first computer game that he had ever played. In that game, a ninja made his way through the Japanese countryside, the palace grounds and a castle to rescue a princess. At every level, the ninja had obstacles of increasing difficulty. He remembered the final challenge. “Gentlemen,” Jamail announced with a confident expression, “it’s time to assault the inner sanctum.”

The top of the eighth inning started badly for Clemens. The first two batters reached on a walk and a single putting runners on first and third with no outs. With only a one run lead and K. pitching the way he was, if East Timor scored, the game was probably lost. In the command center, Jamail got the word from Giuliani that he had been waiting for. “We have found their headquarters.”

"Great!" Jamail responded, "break down the door and kick their sorry asses out onto the street."

"We have a little problem," Rudy answered. "Somehow, the American Civil Liberties Union got wind of this. They won't let us proceed without a warrant. The police are escorting a judge to the site as we speak. You need to stall for a couple of minutes."

A rummy Billy Gates started to scream into the mike, "Oh shit, just break the fucking door down!" but a calm Jamail cut him off. "Please move as fast as you can. I have a plan."

With that, Jamail contacted Bob Sheppard. "Plan B," he said. Next, he buzzed Lashman Singh. "The goose is in the meadow," he said in code. "Time to let out the fox."

A sleepy Peter Norton rushed to the command chair. "What the hell is going on? Why don't we know about Plan B?"

"Apparently, you didn't get the memo," Jamail said in a mocking tone. "Now sit down and be quiet. I have a job to do."

"Ladies and gentlemen," Bob Sheppard announced in his famous slow and deliberate manner, today even slower and more deliberate, "we are fortunate to have a distinguished guest at the ballpark, a man who has become famous using science to better the lives of the poor and down-trodden from all over the planet, a man who has never rested in his quest to make the world a better place. Would you please stand and give a warm New York welcome to Professor Lashman Singh."

With that, the baseball data on the scoreboard disappeared and was replaced by Singh's logo, which slowly transformed into a giant picture of the professor. Simultaneously, Singh walked onto the field from a door behind home plate. He was followed by a gaggle of disciples dressed in togas and robes, behind them an adoring mass of gorgeous young women. As he approached the microphone set up at home plate, there was one thing for certain, Professor Singh knew how to make an entrance.

In their box, Steve Glickman and Garden Bostwick were getting riled. They understood exactly what the stalling tactic was all about. Pushing past the bevy of call girls surrounding them, they raced down to the field screaming at the umpires to take control. Their voices were drowned out by the fake applause that Professor Singh had arranged to be piped through the stadium's speakers.

Meanwhile, outside a nondescript crack house in the Bronx, Judge Judy, who was still technically appointed to the New York district court, arrived on the premises. The ACLU tried to object, but Judy, who was a long time baseball fan, quickly signed a warrant. Immediately, the DEA team comprised of real officers as well as Giuliani, Tom Cruise, Jennifer Stone, Tiger Woods and Paris Hilton crashed down the door and stormed the building. Cruise knew exactly what he was doing. He had stormed buildings in almost half of his movies. The only one that looked out of place was Paris Hilton. Paris was wearing a cop uniform that her private tailor had worked on all through the night. Scant and tight fitting, Paris looked like a cop from a low budget porn movie. That didn't stop her from finding the cutest looking of all the East Timor technicians. Telling him to get up against the wall, she handcuffed him and led him out of the building where her publicist was waiting with a personal photographer. "The National Enquirer will pay a fortune for these photos," she thought to herself.

The East Timor techies, mostly twenty-something kids from MIT, were led from the building. Peter Norton's people, led by Allison Brown, a top assistant, took over the computers and started typing furiously. In the command center, Jamail got the message he had been waiting for. "We have assumed command and control," Allison pronounced. "The Snemelcs are ours!"

Meanwhile, behind home plate, Lashman Singh was starting to read his speech from a thick folder that he had placed on the podium. "Good people of the planet earth," he said in his high-pitched voice. "At this great stadium…"

Before he could go any further, his microphone went dead. Bob Sheppard had got the word from Jamail to resume play. "Thank you, Professor Singh, for honoring us with your presence. Now it is time to play ball." With that, the professor was ushered back to the tunnel and off the field. As he disappeared from view, he threw his speech onto the ground. "Fucking baseballers," he said under his breath.

With Allison Brown controlling the transmissions, Clemens was able to strike out Snemelcs E., F. and G. East Timor stranded two runners, and the game moved to the bottom of the eighth with the all-stars still leading by one run.

George Steinbrenner, relieved and almost giddy, opened the refrigerator in his sky box and uncorked a bottle of champagne. "Brian," he said turning to his general manager, "get my CPA on the phone and find out if I would have to pay taxes on the $1,000,000,000."

In the dugout, the players were beaming as if they all had been given a new lease on life. In the command center, the team was re-energized. Only Jamail had a concerned look on his face. A relieved Billy Gates looked like a man that just found out his spouse had taken the day off and wasn't in the World Trade Center on September 11. He caught Jamail's concerned look out of the corner of his eye and walked over to him at the bridge. "What's the matter?" he asked. "We have control of their players."

"Mr. Gates," Jamail replied, "we have breached the inner sanctum, but we haven't dealt with the final challenge. I am sure that there is a kill switch."

"What the hell is a kill switch?" Gates yelled at the top of his voice. The room went silent. Everyone turned towards Jamail with a blank look on their faces awaiting his explanation.

Chapter 28

"Every video game has a final challenge. In *Revenge of the Ninja*, the Kung Fu master appears out of nowhere just before you save the princess. In *Raceway 2006*, you run out of gas just before the finish line. In *Superman Returns*, kryptonite robs you of your power before you defeat Lex Luthor. In the vernacular, we call that the 'kill switch' because if you don't see it coming, just when you start to smell victory, you die and lose the game. Everything that I have seen about East Timor tells me that there must be a kill switch."

By now, the members of Bill Gates' tech team were exhausted and unable to think or concentrate. They couldn't grasp what the young wizard was talking about. Jamail, on the other hand, was focused and energized as if he had just awoken from a ten-hour sleep. The night before, Gates had asked him how he stayed alert for such long periods of time. "It's what I do Mr. Gates," Jamail had explained. "Video game competitions often last three days without a break."

When the bottom of the eighth got underway, Tankai Lu was still in control of transmissions to the East Timor players. Allison Brown had opened a portal that allowed Lu to operate the East Timor computers from his workstation in the stadium command center. Ichiro settled into the batters box. As K. wound up for the first delivery, Tankai shot 20,000 bytes of conflicting data into the pitcher's glasses. The pitch sailed wide for ball one. For the next pitch, the programmer changed the codes, ball two. Tankai was having fun. The rest of the room started to relax. The third offering was in the dirt, ball three. "Watch this," Tankai bragged. "I am going to program an intentional ball." With a smirk on his face, he hit a series of strokes on his keyboard. K. wound up and threw. The ball hit the catcher's mitt so hard that smoke came out of the glove. The sound of impact reached every corner of the ballpark. The radar gun on the scoreboard read one hundred and twenty miles per hour. Strike one!

George Steinbrenner gasped and spilled his champagne on the floor. Billy Gates, now almost comatose, took a cold glass of water and splashed it against his face. Tankai started to pound his keyboard. "What's going on?" Peter Norton screamed into his ear.

"I don't know. I seem to have lost control," Tankai replied.

"Try again," Norton ordered.

"It's no use," Tankai said. "It doesn't matter what key I hit. I am frozen. Someone has compromised my computer. Look at my screen."

Sure enough, as the room crowded around Tankai's computer, a video cartoon appeared. A stripper was doing a pole dance to some awful music. After about twenty seconds of removing her clothes, the stripper was gone, and Steve Glickman's face appeared in her place. "Please make my check payable in dollars or any other hard currency," he said with a wry, disrespectful look on his face. "See you at the post-game press conference."

Everyone turned their attention to Jamail. Gates was the first to speak. "What the hell is going on, and what do we do next?"

"Our opponents just hit the kill switch," Jamail said with the same steady look on his face. "They have eliminated all contact with the players from any and all sources. Now everybody step back and give me some room. It's time to contest the zenith. We have arrived at the final level."

It took two more fastballs for K. to strike out Ichiro. Jeter and A-Rod looked at three strikes each for the next two outs. Going into the top of the ninth, the all-stars were still up one to nothing, but no one was confident. The Snemelcs were now playing at top capacity, better than in the previous two games. Transmissions were blocked, and they were on autopilot. There was nothing anyone could do. In the field box, Glickman turned to Garden Bostwick, "There is no mercy rule in the top of the ninth. Let's run the score up to fifty before we stop. We won't give the signal to quit until every fan has left the ballpark." With that, he waited until the television camera turned on him. With a phony grin on his face, he lit an oversized cigar.

Jamail buzzed Tommy Lasorda and explained the situation. "You are on your own, Mr. Lasorda. There is nothing we can do now." The old manager thought for a second and then turned to address his players. He chose his words carefully, "All bets are off. The geeks have turned off the computers. It's up to us to put them down on our own."

He walked over to his pitcher. Clemens stood up and took the ice pack off his arm. "How are you feeling Rocket?" Tommy asked. "Mariano is ready in the bull pen."

"Skip," Clemens replied, "to answer your question, I feel like an old shit that has been through the wringer one time too many, but no one is going to take me out of this game."

With that, the Rocket stepped on to the field. This would be the last inning that he would ever pitch. It didn't matter if his arm hurt, or if it fell off his shoulder. It was time to leave it all on the field.

Snemelc A. tapped his spikes and stepped into the batters box.

Clemens first pitch was a splitter. Snemelc A. drove it 600 feet over the left field foul pole. Fortunately, there was a slight right to left breeze in the ballpark, and the umpire signaled foul ball.

In the owners box, George Steinbrenner noticed the scoreboard indicating that the last offering was Clemens' one hundred and fiftieth pitch. He grabbed his hotline to the command center. Jamail picked up the phone, "Yes, Mr. Steinbrenner."

"I need to talk to Mr. Gates, now!" the Boss screamed.

"Mr. Gates has put me in charge sir," Jamail said politely. "You can talk to me."

"Tell Lasorda to get Clemens out of the game. He's got nothing left. They're going to kill him. He's thrown one hundred and fifty pitches. No one has ever thrown that many in the history of the game. Do it…"

All of a sudden, Jamail had an idea. He hung up the phone on Steinbrenner and switched the connection to Tommy. "Don't let Roger throw another pitch," he said in a calm voice. "Go the mound. Tell him to walk the next three batters. Tell him to throw every intentional ball as hard as he can."

Lasorda started to say something about never walking the tying run to first base, but Jamail cut him off, "Trust me, Mr. Lasorda. Just do it. Tell Roger to walk the bases loaded and then rear back and throw his best stuff right down Broadway."

The manager started to ask Jamail whose side he was on, but thought better of it. In his heart, he knew that his team didn't have a chance playing straight up. He called time and walked slowly to the mound. As he walked, he wasn't sure what he was going to say when he got there.

CHAPTER 29

Billy Gates strode over to Jamail. "What is your plan?" he asked.

"Well, Mr. Gates," Jamail replied with calm look on his face. "I have a theory. It's a long shot, but it's the only idea that I have. Mr. Steinbrenner said that no pitcher in Major League history has ever thrown one hundred and fifty pitches in a game. You told me that the Timor Institute of Technology and Sports has loaded every game into their database, but no one has ever thrown one hundred and fifty pitches during that time. I don't know what Roger's arm will do, but it is bound to act a little different, maybe the difference between a home run and a long fly. Besides, Clemens is already a little unstable. After being told to walk the bases loaded with a one run lead in the ninth inning, there is no telling what he will do. The uncertainty gives us the element of surprise."

Billy Gates stared at the young gaming master. He was impressed. His plan might not work, but it was creative thinking. "Impressive work," the entrepreneur thought to himself. He always put a premium on creativity from his associates.

Jamail continued, "Besides, it is the only thing we have to go on, and it gives us about five minutes to come up with the true McGuffin." McGuffin was a term that gamers used. It had its roots back to Alfred Hitchcock who claimed that every great movie had a McGuffin that created suspense and intrigue. The McGuffin was always visible throughout the whole movie, right in front of everyone's eyes, but only the hero could figure it out.

Jamail looked around the room full of tired geniuses all of whom had just about given up hope. Only he was still focused and optimistic. He chose his words carefully, "Gentlemen, every character has a vulnerability and every puzzle a solution. The Scarecrow was afraid of fire. The Wicked Witch was melted with water. In the War of the Worlds, the aliens were defeated by bacteria. If one hundred and fifty pitches doesn't do the trick, and it might not, we have five minutes to come up with the true McGuffin, or we lose, and I have never lost a game yet. We need ideas, and we need them fast." He looked down on the field where Roger Clemens was having a heated discussion with Tommy Lasorda. It looked like the Rocket was getting ready to punch his manager in the mouth. Derek Jeter was trying to talk him down, and the home plate umpire, who had originally come to the mound to break up the conference, was standing between them. "Think people, think," Jamail urged.

Just then, the door to the command center opened, and a security guard walked in. "Professor Singh needs to talk to you," he said.

"Not now," Gates said, "we are a little busy."

"He is insistent," the guard replied.

"Tell him to come back tomorrow if he can bring us the broomstick of the Wicked Witch of the West," Peter Norton said sarcastically.

The guard turned to leave the room, but the enraged professor charged through the door. He had heard Norton's comments and was furious.

"You fucking assholes," the Professor screamed, "I am sick and tired of being treated like some trivial accessory. I am Professor Lashman Singh. I am world famous for handling problems far greater than this stupid American game of baseball. I won't be dismissed like some arm candy while you self-proclaimed geniuses act like a bunch of little school girls."

The security guard stepped in to forcibly eject the Professor from the room. He grabbed Singh by the arm and just about had him out the door when Jamail stood up from the command chair. "Wait a moment," he said, "that's brilliant. I think I have an idea." He looked down to the field where the Rocket was issuing an intentional walk. With each pitch he screamed, grunted, and hurled the ball with all his strength into Pudge's mitt. With each pitch, his fury was building.

Chapter 30

Jamail continued, “I think Professor Singh is on to something, the one thing we have overlooked, the most heinous insult that can be directed at a baseball player of any age. From the first day of Little League to rookie year in the pros, when someone wants to put a ball player down, when they want to unnerve him, when they want to start a fist fight, they simply pronounce ‘he throws like a girl’ or ‘he swings the bat like a little school girl’ or ‘he slides like a girl with a cake in her pocket’. Thank you Professor Singh for such profound insight. I think we can use it to our advantage.” Jamail turned to Billy Gates, “If Clemens can’t do it after one hundred and sixty-two pitches, we need to get a girl on the mound.”

One of the techs in the back of the room yelled, “Jenny Finch is here. She’s doing the game on the Lifetime network. I saw her in the hotel lobby last night.”

Everyone in the room knew who she was. Jenny Finch, the six foot two blonde bombshell, the famed softball pitcher, ace of the U.S. Olympic team, was quite possibly the fastest windmiller who ever lived. If there was any doubt that she was the best softball pitcher, there was no doubt that she was most beautiful.

Jamail sensed the kill. In a measured tone, he ordered, “Get her in a uniform and get her to the bullpen quickly. We still have some work to do.”

A gleaming Professor Singh adjusted his turban. “It’s about time these people show me the respect I am entitled to,” he thought to himself.

On the field, Clemens finished walking Snemelc C. The bases were loaded. If looks could have killed, anyone coming near the mound would have been a dead man. The Rocket’s right hand was now covered with blood. His arm hung from his side like a limp rag. Jamail’s idea was brilliant. No one had ever batted against a pitcher that was so wasted. The East Timorean batters had no data for it, and the kill switch had destroyed all on field communication. Jamail held his breath. He knew that gaming was about instinct and taking chances, but there was a lot riding on this decision. Snemelc D. walked to the plate. Clemens pounded the ball into his mitt.

Meanwhile, Jenny Finch was being escorted to the bullpen. A clubhouse attendant would meet her there with a special uniform. There would be a pink rose pinned over the number. Jamail didn’t know why he ordered that, but for some reason, he thought that it would be a nice touch.

Clemens wound up and threw. Snemelc D. swung. There was a deafening crack of the bat. Billy Gates, George Steinbrenner and the rest of the crew closed their eyes. They couldn’t bear to look. Only Jamail could keep his eyes on the field. What he saw was a screaming line drive that looked like it was heading to right field. Jose Reyes, the second baseman, leapt, and at the very top of his leap, he snagged the liner, the play of the century. A quick toss to Jeter and Snemelc B. was doubled up off second base. What could have been a three run disaster turned into a double play. East Timor had runners on first and third, but there were two outs in the top of the ninth, and they were still trailing by a run.

In his box, Steve Glickman pushed one of the trophy girls off his arm and whispered something to Guffy. Guffy had his head in his hands. His expression was utter disbelief. The dumbest looking girl in the box tried to cheer them up. “That’s baseball, a game of inches,” she squeaked.

“$1,000,000,000 an inch to be precise,” Guffy responded.

Back in the command center, Jamail’s mind was in overdrive. “So much for the one hundred and sixty pitch theory,” Jamail thought out loud. “Is Finch ready yet?” He had temporarily lost track of time.

“Not even close,” the bullpen coach said. “She’s putting on her uniform. She says she will need fifteen minutes to warm up.”

Jamail hailed Lasorda on the two way. “Mariano time,” he instructed the manager. “Get him in the game. Tell him to walk the next batter. Tell him to do it slowly. We are stalling for time.” Lasorda didn’t ask any questions. He hopped up the dugout stairs and took his time ambling out to the mound. Clemens didn’t want to leave, but when he finally handed Tommy the ball, he walked off the field to the loudest and longest standing ovation in Yankee history. Lasorda gave him a big hug instead of the usual pat on the butt. To kill time, Tommy had him go out for three curtain calls.

Billy Gates paced back and forth next the bridge. As the inning progressed, he was gaining great admiration for Jamail’s ability to stay calm as he handled the crisis. “If we get through this on good terms,” he thought to himself, “there might be a position for this young man at Microsoft. Who knows, with me retiring in a few years…?” Then he snapped back to reality. He must concentrate. It was still the ninth inning.

Mariano Rivera was surprised and a little hurt when told that he was being brought in to stall and then to walk a batter, but Mariano was the ultimate team player. He would do whatever was asked to help his team win. If Clemens was the road warrior, Mariano was the consummate professional. While Clemens was the best starting pitcher in his generation, Mariano was the best closer ever.

In his box, a rejuvenated Steve Glickman started licking his chops. He knew that every one of his players was fully programmed to bat against Rivera. The closer's entrance in the ninth inning had been predictable and had therefore been thoroughly prepared for. The result would be inevitable. Victory was in the bag. When Mariano threw the first pitch for a ball, so far from the plate that E. couldn't reach it, Glickman's facial expression went from ecstasy to panic. He whispered again into Guffy's ear. They stood up and scurried to a concession stand in the mezzanine where they pulled out their cell phones and started shouting instructions.

Mariano played his part to perfection. On every pitch, he shook off several signs before throwing an intentional ball. Between every pitch, he made two or three pick off attempts at first base even though C. was standing on the base with no lead. After ball two, Lasorda came out to the mound for a conference, and stayed there until the umpire ordered him back. After ball three, A-Rod got something in his eye. It took the trainer a couple of minutes to get it out.

Just before ball four, Jamail saw the bullpen coach take off his hat, the universal sign. Jenny Finch was ready.

Jamail spoke to Bob Sheppard in the public address booth, "Everything is in order. No need to go to plan C."

Gates was impressed that Jamail even had a plan C. Looking over the gamer's shoulder, he noticed some notes on his pad. Under the heading plan C was scribbled, second stall, Captain Bligh, tribute to East Timor legacy, Little Richard. There were additional notes under the headings Plan D, E, F and G. Gates knew better than to ask any questions. Jamail was on a roll. It was no time to break his stride.

As Snemelc E. headed to first with a free pass, Mariano Rivera walked slowly off the mound. Over the PA, Bob Sheppard announced, "Now pitching for the all-stars, Jennifer Finch."

Chapter 31

Snemelc L. came running out of the East Timor dugout to protest. "We're playing the Major League all-stars. She isn't an all-star. She isn't even in the Major Leagues," he shouted as he kicked dirt and gestured with his hands.

Tommy Lasorda came on to the field to keep tabs on the situation. He stood back a few steps ready to intervene if necessary. The umpires ruled that this was an exhibition with an unlimited roster. Jennifer Finch could pitch. L. turned to leave the field. Still agitated, he kicked some dirt when he passed Lasorda. Tommy must have said something to him, because Snemelc stepped up to the all-star manager and started yelling. The two stood toe to toe, their faces less than three inches apart, screaming into each other's face. The crowd came to their feet. Team East Timor might have been prepared to pitch or bat against any Major League player, but there was nothing in their regimen that prepared them to do verbal battle with Tommy Lasorda. As they continued to yell at each other, it became obvious to the crowd's delight, that Lasorda was getting his points across very explicitly. After they were finally separated and heading back to their respective benches, L. seemed upset, almost despondent, while Tommy had a triumphant look on his face. He walked off the field to another standing ovation. As he stepped down into the dugout, the all-stars were bouncing up and down, proud of their manager. Every player gave him five as if he just hit a walk-off game seven grand slam. The first question addressed to Tommy in the post-game press conference was "What did he say in that argument?" More on that later.

Jenny Finch and Pudge Rodriguez had a short meeting on the mound. Pudge trotted back behind the plate. Finch windmilled and delivered. The ball started low, skimming the earth, and broke up toward the catcher's mitt, a perfect pitch, strike one. Snemelc E. didn't move his bat. Softball players are used to a ball thrown underhand instead of overhand. Curves break up instead of down. Pitchers throw risers instead of splitters. If an average college softball player batted against Jenny Finch throwing from a Major League sixty feet instead of forty-six feet, they would have hit the ball easily, but nothing in the history of baseball had prepared East Timor for this latest wrinkle.

Jenny delivered again, this time a changeup that fluttered in the air and dropped into Pudge's mitt. The home plate umpire sensing the magnitude of the unfolding drama put some extra gusto into his signal, strike two. The crowd came to their feet, the clamor so loud that you couldn't talk to the person standing next to you. Glickman and Guffy disappeared from sight into the tunnel between the mezzanine and the exit concourse. Jennifer Stone, whose job was now to keep tabs on the enemy, paged the command center on her wrist radio, "Elvis is leaving the building. I'm on his tail."

"Roger that," Jamail responded. Stone headed down the tunnel a measured pace behind her marks. She looked perfect for her part. Wearing a low cut blouse, a trench coat and a pork pie hat, she resembled an Acme detective straight from Central Casting.

In the owners box, Steinbrenner was starting to hyperventilate.

Brian Cashman, afraid his Boss might stroke out, was massaging his back to keep him calm.

In the command center, Jamail contacted Tommy Lasorda. "E. will swing at this pitch no matter what. He doesn't want to strike out looking. Tell her to throw it in the dirt or way outside."

"One step ahead of you," Tommy replied. "I have already given the signal. We've got him set up. Leave this one to me."

With that, Jenny windmilled and threw. The crowd held its breath. You could hear the wind whipping up the flags in centerfield. The pitch was ten feet over E.'s head. E. took a mighty swing. Dust flew from the batters box. Strike three! The crowd started to cheer, but wait, the game wasn't over. The pitch was thrown so far out of the strike zone, that Rodriguez was unable to reach it. The ball sailed over his head towards the backstop. In baseball, a batter and runners can advance on a dropped third strike. In one of the most infamous plays in baseball history, Dodger catcher Mickey Owen dropped a third strike allowing Tommy Heinrich of the Yankees to reach first in the 1941 World Series. Joe Dimaggio singled, and George Keller followed with a double. The Yankees won the game and the championship.

Pudge sprinted to retrieve the ball as it bounced off the back wall. He fired a strike to Finch who was sprinting towards the plate. At the same time, Snemelc A., bolting home from third slid headfirst. The play was close. Every eye in the ballpark, every fan in every bar and every living room in the world focused on Charlie Rutherford waiting for the umpire to make the call. The crowd was silent, and then, the right arm went up in the air. "Yeer OUUUUT!" the umpire yelled, and with that, the game was over.

The all-stars raced onto the field for the traditional dog pile on the pitcher's mound. Every player jumped on top of the pile as it grew higher and higher. Tommy Lasorda even tried to jump to the top before rolling off to the ground. In the East Timor dugout, the players just sat and watched not knowing how to act. This was the first game they had ever lost.

In the owner's box, the champagne began to flow. Steinbrenner turned to Cashman. The first words out of his mouth were, "A billion should buy quite a pitching staff next year, Santana, Halladay, Zito. Theo Epstein eat your heart out."

In the command center, there were mixed reactions. The young techies were doing cartwheels. Billy Gates and Peter Norton slumped onto the sofa. Lashman Singh was on his cell phone talking to his business agent. Only Jamail continued to manage the post-game with the same level demeanor.

At the same time, an armed detail was escorting Pierre Stahl and his attaches to the boardroom to settle the escrow.

Jim Grey was down on the field. Ignoring the winning all-stars, he was poking his mike into the face of any Snemelc Regor that he could get close to. "East Timor," he said to the network feed, "was the real story." No matter what question Jim Grey asked, every Snemelc's reply was identical, "I am not going to Disneyland. I wouldn't go there if it was the last theme park in the world." The responses puzzled the reporter. The attempt at humor was lost on anyone unaware of Guffy's previous history with the company.

Chapter 32

There were two post-game press conferences. The first one, the traditional conference, had mikes set up for each manager, the starting pitchers, and players selected from each club. This conference occupied the larger of the two pressrooms in Yankee stadium. The room was crowded with reporters from all the major media organizations. Tommy Lasorda arrived first, followed by Roger Clemens. The Rocket had his arm in a sling covered with several ice packs. Jennifer Finch walked in next. Derek Jeter was the last of the all-stars to arrive. The press waited for the East Timor players and management. After a couple of minutes, the conference started without them.

Jim Grey raised his hand first, but the players on the podium ignored him. He had served his usefulness and was again one of the enemy. Baseball players universally disdained him for a lifetime of thoughtless comments culminating with his infamous interview of Pete Rose.

The first question was directed at Tommy Lasorda by Sam Borden of the Daily News. "What did you say to East Timor's manager in the ninth inning?"

Lasorda wasn't bashful with his answer. "He told me he was going to complain to the tournament commissioner and get Jennifer disqualified. He said that they would play the game under protest, and they would be declared the winner. I told him that I had been threatened by experts many times, so it didn't bother me to be threatened by a bush league clone son of a bitch in a lime green uniform that didn't deserve to have the same name as a great pitcher even if it was spelled backwards."

"Thanks, Tommy," Borden said. He scribbled some notes while cameras clicked and flashbulbs popped.

Anthony McCarran of the Daily News directed the next question to Roger Clemens. "Rocket, what did you think of the East Timor batters?"

That question had been asked at almost every post-game press conference in baseball history. The generic answer was to complement the opposition for a game well played. No pitcher ever wanted to give a batter extra motivation the next time they met. Roger, on the other hand, was done with baseball. He would never face East Timor again. "I think they were a bunch of shit kicking ass holes," Roger answered. He had always wanted to say something like that to the press. "I just wish I had enough left to finish the game. It will give me great pleasure to think that they will have a miserable thirty hour flight back to East Timor or wherever they came from."

The second press conference was starting in the smaller room across the hall. Lashman Singh was the sole interviewee on the podium. The press chairs were occupied by a number of his followers. A video camera directed in such a way as to make the room look full recorded a number of pre-rehearsed questions and answers for the professor's upcoming documentary. A young, bald Tibetan man wearing a Yankee jacket with a fake press pass around his neck, raised his hand and stood up. "Professor Singh, how did you know that they wouldn't be able to hit Finch?" he asked.

Singh scratched his beard and pointed a finger first to his head and then to his heart. After giving the camera a few seconds to absorb his brilliance, he spoke, ignoring the question that had been posed, "Human triumph is the alliance of power of the brain and passion of the heart. The epic of man is defined by great minds dissecting problems and solving them." He went on to speak for twenty minutes until the camera ran out of film.

While both conferences were concluding, Pierre Stahl and his escorts reached the Yankee boardroom. There was still the matter of settling the wager.

Chapter 33

George Steinbrenner had assembled his whole team for the escrow ceremony. The plan was to take care of business and then throw a party to celebrate the conquest. Tiger Woods, Paris Hilton, Tom Cruise, Billy Gates and Peter Norton sat on one side of the big polished oak table. Brian Cashman and Rudy Giuliani sat next to George at the head. Seats were reserved for Tommy Lasorda, Jim Grey, Lashman Singh and Jennifer Stone. Some of the senior technicians and a few special reporters had been invited to sit in chairs behind the table against the wall. Otherwise, it was an "A" list group by invitation only. Donald Trump and David Letterman had to call in favors for an invite.

Pierre Stahl sat at the other end of the table with his briefcase in front of him. On each side were big Swiss guards. Next to them sat company lawyers. After a couple of minutes of small talk, George Steinbrenner, who never really liked small talk, was getting impatient. "Well let's get rolling, boys," he said in a loud voice that had been strained by nine innings of anxiety.

"Proper form would be to wait for all principals," Stahl replied courteously but firmly. His fingers twirled the ends of his handlebar moustache.

"East Timor might take a pass," Brian Cashman cut in. "They probably don't think much of our company. We don't have to wait for them anyway."

“Two more minutes,” Stahl replied, “then we will start not withstanding their default.”

Jamail Hawthorne walked into the room. One by one, the team acknowledged the young gamer. Steinbrenner had him come up to the head of the table. He had the Yankees’ photographer snap some pictures of the two of them standing next to the official trophy. With all excitement of the wagers surrounding the event, the trophy presented by Baseball Commissioner, Bud Selig had almost become an afterthought.

The champagne and hors d’oeuvres were starting to circulate. The room was full of smiling people. Only Jamail seemed a little reserved. Billy Gates wondered if maybe the young man knew something that the rest of them didn’t.

A Yankee assistant announced that the press conferences were over. Tommy Lasorda, Lashman Singh and Roger Clemens were on their way up. Steve Glickman and Garden Bostwick III were still nowhere to be seen.

“We will start as soon as those three arrive,” Stahl announced. He took a key from his pocket and removed the handcuffs from the briefcase and his wrist. From the case, he removed a lap top computer and a stack of legal papers. From his inside suit pocket, he removed a small portfolio of codes.

By the time Stahl finished sorting his papers, the final guests, with the exception of Glickman and Bostwick, had arrived. Clemens and Lasorda were wearing caps and tee shirts proclaiming them victors in baseball’s ‘good will’ tournament. His right arm still in a sling, the Rocket had a beer in his left hand. Tommy had a beer in each hand. It looked like he had downed two or three more before he got there.

Professor Singh had waited for Clemens and Lasorda to enter first so that he could be the last to arrive. Much to his dismay, no one paid him any due. In fact, Billy Gates in a very uncharacteristic move, had paid a couple of the assistants to pretend that they didn't recognize the professor and demand to see his credentials. Gates smiled as Singh turned beet red before producing his pass.

Pierre Stahl took charge of the meeting. "Thank you gentlemen, for allowing the United Bank of Switzerland to be at your service. My first act will be to return all pledge documents to the victors. Mr. Steinbrenner, in this folder, you will find your quitclaim deed to the New York Yankees, your personal check for $500,000,000, your loan papers at Citibank and all of the documents perfecting the liens on your personal property and other collateral."

A UBS page took the folder and handed it to the Yankee owner. While Brian Cashman quickly examined all of the documents and stamped them 'Void', Steinbrenner raised a glass of champagne. "Gentleman, we have made arrangements to present all of these documents to the archives at the Baseball Hall of Fame. I want to thank each and every one of you for your role in making this conquest possible."

Professor Singh stood up to make a second toast, but Pierre Stahl ignored him and continued, "Next, by pushing this button, I will transfer $1,000,000,000 from the special account set up by the East Timor government to Mr. Steinbrenner's personal operating account." He hit the button. He paused a second to allow the transaction to execute. He pushed the button a second time, then a third. There was a puzzled look on his face. "This is most unusual," he pronounced. "Somehow, the computer is telling me that the account is empty. Of course, that would not be possible. The account has been protected by multiple firewalls and the full encryptions of UBS security."

George Steinbrenner put down his glass, "Didn't East Timor have to pledge oil reserves as collateral?"

"They certainly did," Stahl answered. "We will exercise on the collateral." He hit another button on his computer. Nothing happened. "This is most unusual," he mumbled for a second time. "I'm sure that there is nothing to worry about, but the computer is telling me that all the collateral was released an hour ago."

"But I will still get paid," Steinbrenner demanded, "UBS is on the line as the escrow agent?"

"Of course, you have always had our personal guarantee," Stahl replied. Then, one of the young UBS lawyers in the group whispered something in his ear. Stahl stood up. "We need to leave immediately to begin an investigation of this matter."

"Do I get my money or not?" Steinbrenner pressed.

"The investigation will get our full attention."

"What the fuck does that mean?" Steinbrenner was losing his calm.

Just then, a Yankee office assistant rushed into the room. He handed a note to Brian Cashman.

"What now?" Steinbrenner shouted.

"Apparently, there has been a coup d'état in East Timor. The prime minister has taken control of the royal palace. He has issued a statement that for the good of the people of East Timor, all government assets have been seized, and all contracts of the previous administration have been repudiated."

Steinbrenner started shouting orders, "Where the fuck are Glickman and Bostwick? Get my lawyers on the phone. Call the airports and keep those assholes from leaving the country." Just then, Stahl noticed that a video was starting to run on his computer. Everyone crowded around the screen. The video had a close up of Glickman's face as he started talking. "Did you idiots really think that your sniveling old technology was a match for mine? The games were a blast. My compliments to Jamail. He was a worthy opponent. The rest of you are really quite sad. Mr. Stahl, if I were you, I would have your company IT people check portals 178 through 187. It took us about two minutes to break through your bank's security. Mr. Lasorda and the rest of you baseball people, you will never learn how we developed the perfect ballplayer. Actually, I don't think that your simple minds could handle the truth. As we speak, a fire has started that will destroy all of the records at the Timor Institute of Technology and Sports. The only copies remaining are in my possession. By the way, Mr. Bostwick and I have decided not to attend your little post-game shindig. We have decided to move our operation. I am sure that you will understand if I don't give you the precise location. Please think good thoughts for us. Who knows, you might hear from us sometime again. Oh, I almost forgot, Ms. Stone, what a lovely lady. You will find her in the ladies restroom grandstand level behind first base. Don't worry, the immobilizer glob is quite harmless. It was invented by some colleagues of mine at MIT for the army. Ta ta and toot a lou." With that, the screen went blank, and the computer started to fizzle.

"Very impressive," Jamail thought to himself.

EPILOGUE

Gambling debts are often referred to as 'debts of honor' because there is no legal means to collect on them if the loser decides not to pay. George Steinbrenner's attorneys worked through the night examining all the papers from the escrow file. By the day's end, they concluded that the Yankee owner had no legal leg to stand on. The oil reserves were the property of the East Timorean people. The former leaders had no authority to pledge them. The money that had been deposited with UBS had been rerouted twenty-six times in the three minutes after Steve Glickman had broken through the firewall. It had sat for about half an hour in a Cayman Island account in the name of Fogies and Fools at the Old Suckers Bank. The bank didn't actually exist and all of the ABA numbers had been bogus. From there, the money had been withdrawn and routed back to East Timor in the name of the new ruling party. The new president was not willing to relinquish any of it. The Timor Institute of Technology and Sports had gone up in smoke. All the records, scientists and athletes had disappeared and were nowhere to be found.

"But I was willing to pay them," Steinbrenner whined to his lawyers.

"That just proves that you are a man of honor," his lawyers replied.

"Or a damn fool," Steinbrenner thought to himself.

The Boss soon got over his malaise. He remembered what a wealthy old fisherman had once told him when George was complaining that he was only worth one billion.

"Stop whining George," the fisherman had said. "I am only worth fifty million, and there really isn't much that you can do with your billion that I can't do with my fifty million. Besides, you have twenty times more to worry about."

There is a saying that men with good wives are happy, and men with bad wives are philosophers. George became philosophic. "After all, we beat the crap out of them and saved the Yankees," he kept telling himself. As Spring Training approached, his thoughts moved on to the pursuit of another World Series championship.

Jennifer Stone never got over being outwitted by the marks she was tailing. Glickman had been sure that she would follow them and had been prepared. Just at the moment she passed the ladies room by the grandstand, he had looked around knowing that she would duck through the door to stay out of sight. He had paid one of the custodial crew fifty bucks to drop a little pill into a wash sink filled with water. In an instant, the tablet expanded into a soft growing, sticky gob that filled the whole room and pinned Jennifer into one of the toilet stalls. She was stuck there until the New York Fire Department cut her loose. Her reputation suffered effectively ending her career as a private eye. Within a few months, she was back on her feet as a celebrity spokesperson for infomercials selling everything from perfume to exercise machines. One day, she vanished suddenly. The only clues to her disappearance were a receipt for a one way ticket to Caracas and credit card slips for jungle attire and survival gear.

Billy Gates hired Jamail Hawthorne the next day. Gates wanted to put the young gamer in charge of his whole Xbox division, but Jamail wasn't interested. They settled on the job of gaming test pilot. For the next thirty years, no game would be released to the public before Jamail played it, tested it and refined it. It was the perfect career. Every day, Jamail sat in his special office and played computer games from dawn until dark. One trademark of his reign was that at some point in every game that he approved, an Indian mystic appeared. Sometimes the mystic wore a turban. Sometimes he was disguised. He often had a role solving a key puzzle, but more often than not, his role in the game was purely symbolic. He would utter some profound words or philosophic thoughts. Those who had been involved in the baseball classic debated whether the mystic was a jester or a hero in honor of Lashman Singh.

Professor Singh was the only team member to parlay his participation into personal riches. The cell phone call he had made immediately following game three was to his patent attorney. Before the umpire signed the official scorecard, Singh had copyrighted the phrase, "The Real World Series." Every time the words were written or spoken in a commercial venue, the professor earned a royalty. Two weeks after the contest, he published a book entitled, "Winning the Real World Series, how Professor Lashman Singh saved the National Pastime." The book contained pictures and quotes from all the meetings that he had compiled with hidden cameras and tape recorders. It quickly became a best seller and to this day is the only first person account of the proceedings.

Steve Glickman and Garden Bostwick III vanished from public life. The last person to see them was Jennifer Stone just before she ducked into the ladies room. Rumors circulated that they moved their operations to the jungles of Venezuela to plan their next conquest. At first, Interpol tried to track them down, but the search was soon abandoned. After all, other than welch on a bet, they hadn't done anything illegal, nor had anyone gotten hurt. In fact, upon reflection, they had given the city of New York and the whole baseball world a pretty exciting spring. They would surface years later having masterminded another diabolical plan aimed at defaming other institutions.

There was a side story that a few astute people connected to Glickman and Bostwick. Later that summer, Disney planned to release their big budget animated movie, "Lamb Chop." The movie was a touching story of a ewe and her baby lamb, Chop, trying to return home after they were kidnapped by an evil trapper. Every time Disney tried to run the film, at some random moment, Chop's sweet voice would be dubbed over by the gruff voice of a drunken sailor spewing one expletive after another. Disney spent millions of dollars on programmers to try to eliminate the problem. However, each time the film was run, the problem resurfaced. The company finally gave up and shelved the project. Somewhere Glickman and Bostwick were smiling.

The End

Another Year in the Bronx

Chapter 1

"Where are you from kid?"

"Pea Patch, West Virginee."

"You mean West Virginia?"

"Yup, West Virginee."

Cletus Barnes, a clubhouse attendant for the New York Yankees, turned and walked toward Joe Torre's office. Cletus was a black man, seventy-some years old. He walked with a limp and a hunched back. The joke in the clubhouse was that he had been around forever. He had no special job. The organization kept him because he had grown on them over the years.

"Mr. Torre, there is a Jethro Bodine from West Virginia that wants to talk to you."

"What's he want Clete?"

"Says he heard that you were looking for a pitcher."

Joe Torre was in no mood for amusement. About once a week, some crank would show up and want to try out. Small people, fat old men, pretty women, they all wanted to play for the Yanks. "Just give me a chance, Joe," they would beg.

Usually, Joe would come out and talk to them. "Thanks kid," he would say. Joe was a decent guy, and even in tough times, he tried to be pleasant, but this had been a bad week. Carl Pavano was on the disabled list. Chien-Ming Wang had a sore shoulder. Last night, Jaret Wright took a batted ball off the neck. To make matters worse, Mike Mussina and Randy Johnson were struggling. The team was in last place with a 13 and 19 record. Tonight, the Red Sox were coming to town. Joe had just gotten off the phone with George Steinbrenner, and the Boss was not happy. It took a lot of energy and patience to humor the Boss. After ten years on the job, he was getting sick of it.

"Tell him that I am sorry, but I'm busy Clete."

"The kid's come a long way to see you Joe."

"Not now. I don't care how you do it, but get rid of him."

"Ok if I let him play catch on the field, Joe? He seems like a nice kid."

"Whatever, just deal with it."

Clete walked back to the kid sitting in the clubhouse."Grab a bat and a ball and let's go work out. Put on that jersey. You can get your picture taken as a Yankee."

Meanwhile in George Steinbrenner's office:

"Mr. Steinbrenner, the Reverend Sharpton is here to see you."

George thought about ducking out the back door but changed his mind. The best way to deal with this was straight on, he thought to himself. The Reverend had been trying to get to see him for weeks now. It was election season, and Al Sharpton needed some time in the spotlight. The door opened, and he came in.

"Al, nice to see you," George said.

"Cut the crap, George. You are never glad to see me."

"Whatever. What can I do for you?"

Nothing Sharpton said would have surprised him. Over the last twenty years, he had seen and heard just about everything. The

Reverend was a nuisance, but nothing that couldn't be dealt with by throwing money in some direction. Throwing money was something that George Steinbrenner was good at. There were very few things or people that George couldn't buy.

"Mr. Steinbrenner, the Yankees are the pride and joy of New York."

"Here it comes," George was thinking.

"Every little child in New York City looks up to your team and wants to be a Yankee." As he continued, he sounded like he was in a pulpit giving a sermon. "You have the chance to be a steamroller for social change." He pounded the table, "but in a city of three million blacks, not one of your coaches, not one of your front office is a Negro."

George started to say that Willy Randolph had been a coach last year, but Sharpton cut him off.

"You have the chance to change history," Sharpton was screaming now. "Be the man and make the change. I can help you rectify the problem." Sharpton paused for effect, "or I can bring the wrath of God and the power of the press down upon you."

George composed himself and looked the reverend in the eyes."Get the fuck out of my office," he said.

Not totally surprised by the reaction, Sharpton smiled. Controversy was good for his reputation. "The picketers will be in front of the stadium tonight. Call me when you want to talk. In feigned indignation, he slammed the door on his way out.

Back in the Yankee clubhouse:

Mel Stottlemyre came running into Joe's office. Joe sensed something was wrong, as Mel rarely got excited. They had been together for many years, some good and some bad. Through all the trials and tribulations, Mel seldom lost his composure. A good man and a good friend, he was a true Yankee and a real gentleman.

"You better get a look at this, Joe. Come on out to the field and have someone bring the Jugs Gun."

"What's going on?" Joe asked.

"You'll have to see for yourself."

The two friends left the office and started down the tunnel to the field. They seemed tired and worn. This season had been more stressful than most. Losing was starting to weigh on them. As they entered the dugout, they could sense excitement. On the mound, Jethro Bodine was warming up. He had a strange awkward windup and an unusual delivery. Around him, the ever present press corps was feverishly talking into their recorders and clicking their camera phones. Derek Jeter, the Yankee captain, was the first one they saw as they came onto the field.

"Who the hell is that kid?" Jeter asked.

"Who you talking about Jetes?"

"That kid on the mound. He is throwing some heavy heat out there."

Cletus came ambling over. "Why that's Mister Jethro Bodine," Cletus said very proud of himself.

"And who the fuck is Jethro Bodine?" Torre asked.

"Just some kid with a one hundred mile an hour heater," Cletus answered.

"No way," Joe thought to himself. The great Nolan Ryan was the last pitcher to break one hundred. Besides, in this day and age, if anyone could throw that fast, the scouts would be all over him." Jethro wound up and threw. Joe and Mel watched and said nothing. Their mouths hung open as if they were dazed.

"Five bucks says it's faster than one hundred," Mel said.

"You're on," Joe replied grabbing the Jugs Gun.

Jethro delivered another pitch. Joe paused for a moment and without saying anything, he reached into his pocket for a five-dollar bill. "Gun must be broken Mel, but I will pay you anyway."

"What's it say Joe?"

"Darn thing says one hundred and twelve."

After several more pitches, they were convinced the gun wasn't broken.

As Joe was listening to Cletus brag about his big discovery, he noticed that Jeter was heading to the batting cage with bat and helmet in hand. The Yankee captain was going to take a couple of whacks against the kid. Jeter, a ten-year major leaguer with a .309 lifetime batting average, was one of the best contact hitters in baseball. Derek walked up to the plate, tapped his bat and took a practice swing. The Yankee brain trust gathered around the cage.

"Take it easy on him, kid," Mel hollered.

Jethro wound up and threw. Jeter didn't have time to start his swing as the ball sped past. Jethro took another ball and pitched again with the same result.

"How's his stuff Jetes?" Torre asked.

Jeter said nothing as he acknowledged Torre with a stare. He dug himself into the batters box. There was a determined look on his face. Jethro threw another pitch.

As the ball sped past the plate, Jeter started his swing. He looked like a Little Leaguer trying to come around against a big league pitcher. Jeter unscrewed himself from the dirt and walked out of the cage.

"I've had enough of that Skip," he said as he headed back to the dugout.

Gary Sheffield was up next. Sheffield was one of the best fastball hitters in the game. He settled in the batters box and prepared for the pitch with his trademark swaggle. Jethro delivered. Sheffield watched a strike right down the middle of the plate. The pitch got Gary's attention. He gritted his teeth and prepared for the next offering. Again, he stood frozen as another fastball sailed right down Broadway. Gary's expression went from amused to serious to pissed off. He tapped his bat and stared at the mound. The next pitch was a high strike over the inside part of the plate. Sheffield didn't even start to swing. His expression went from pissed off to slightly amused to 'I really don't care.' "I've had enough BP for the day," he said matter-of-factly as he passed Joe and headed to the clubhouse. Torre and Stottlemyer walked out to the mound.

"Hey kid, where did you play your ball?"

"In Pea Patch with my brothers."

"How come the scouts never seen ya?"

"We don't have a real field. We never play real games. We just fool around in the back yard."

"Why did you come to New York?"

"Always liked the Yanks, and I heard you really needed a pitcher."

Joe turned to Cletus, "Clete, where is Brian Cashman?"

"He's doing a press conference with Rudy Giuliani."

"Tell him we need to see him."

"He won't be done until one o'clock."

"Cletus," Joe Torre looked at him with a very serious expression, "I don't care if he is making love to Hillary Clinton. Get him down here, NOW."

Chapter 2

Joe Torre sat in his office playing with his lineup card. The last two weeks had been bad, the last two days even worse. Yesterday, the Red Sox had beaten the Yanks with two runs in the ninth. Joe had stuck with his pitcher one batter too long, and neither the Boss nor the press would let him forget it. Today had been a circus. At the news conference to introduce Jethro to the city, Sam Borden of the Daily News nicknamed the prospect the Hillbilly Bomber. The press picked on him so fiercely that Jethro wanted to go home. With his last question, Sam asked if he pitched with or without shoes, and the whole room started laughing. Joe weighed his options. If he started the kid tonight, and he was good, no one would say much, but if Jethro got lit up by the Red Sox, neither he nor the kid would ever live it down. To make matters worse, Steinbrenner had invited Donald Trump to his box for the game. The Boss and The Donald were sharks waiting to feed the press corps with his blood.

Joe penciled Jethro's name in the lineup card, then erased it and penciled it in again. He was in a tight spot. The kid could probably use a tune-up start in the minors, but the press would be all over him if they didn't get to see the 'hillbilly'. "What the hell," he thought to himself, "if he can't do it, I can bring in some other sorry pitcher. Besides, maybe a little comic relief is what this team needs."

That afternoon, Jethro beamed when he was issued his uniform. They had to tailor the sleeves to accommodate his big arms. In the pregame pitching meeting with Mel and catcher Jorge Posada, Jorge asked the kid what he threw.

"Mostly fastballs," the kid said, "and once in a while, a slow ball."

"Do you mean a change?" Jorge asked.

"Yea, a change," Jethro replied.

"No problem," said Mel, always the pragmatist. "Every couple of pitches, just shake your head like your shaking off the sign. That will keep them off balance."

Joe Torre didn't say much during the meeting. Half of him felt bad sending the kid off like a lamb to slaughter. The other half made him smile. It reminded him of when baseball was a game that kids like Jethro played for fun, before it became such a damn serious business.

As game time approached, the knot in Joe's stomach grew. "What the hell," he thought as he walked on the field for the National Anthem. As Ronan Tynan belted out the last few phrases, Joe watched the Red Sox out of the corner of his eye. Manny Ramirez and Johnny Damon were smirking as they watched the big kid finish his warm-up tosses in the bullpen.

"Good evening and welcome to New York Yankees baseball," John Sterling said into the radio microphone. He turned to Susan Waldman, his color man, "What a game we have tonight. The major league debut of Jethro Bodine, the young man from Pea Patch, West Virginia." Then, as an afterthought under his breath, "Shucks, I wonder if he brought his corn cob pipe with him?" His attitude changed after the first pitch to Johnny Damon.

"Strike one!" the umpire cried.

"That pitch came in at over one hundred," Susan Waldman commented quite impressed.

Damon dug into the box, but hardly moved as the next ball sailed into Posada's mitt.

"Strike two."

On the next pitch, Damon took a pathetic, late swing and missed by a mile.

He had struck out on three pitches. As he walked back to the dugout, he wasn't smiling any more.

The next batter was Edgar Renteria. The result was the same. Jethro struck him out easily. Up next came batting champ and MVP candidate, David Ortiz. Ortiz took three mighty swings and headed back to the dugout.

"He struck out the side on nine pitches," Sterling yelled into the mike. "I haven't missed a Yankee game in seventeen years, and I have never seen that."

"He didn't strike them out," Susan Waldman corrected, pausing for emphasis. "He blew them away."

As the Red Sox took the field, and the Yankees came in to bat, Torre noticed that there was a swagger in their gate, something that had been missing of late. Only Jorge Posada came off slowly. He was shaking his catching hand.

Chapter 3

By the fourth inning, the crowd was on its feet. Jethro had struck out eight of his first nine batters, and the Yanks were leading 4 to 0. Only Jason Varitek had reached for the Red Sox with a second inning walk. In the owners box, a beaming George Steinbrenner was showing Donald Trump the grip of the four-seam fastball that his pitcher was throwing. As he had been instructed, Jethro was shaking off signs to fool the batters and throwing nothing but fastballs. In the top of the sixth with two outs, Edgar Renteria tried to bunt on the first pitch and fouled it off. Bodine was not amused. The next pitch, an inside heater hit him square between the shoulder blades. It took Renteria a couple of minutes to shake it off and get down to first base.

"I guess there won't be much more bunting," John Sterling commented.

The rest of the inning was strange. Jethro continued to pitch from the windup with a runner on base. On the first pitch, Renteria stole second unchallenged as Ortiz swung and missed. He took third on a called strike two. Ortiz struck out on a high heater leaving the runner stranded at third.

"First time I ever saw that," Sterling commented.

"There are a lot of things that are happening for the first time tonight," Waldman replied.

In the Daily News Fifth, Sam Borden was the guest in the press box.

"Any comments about this new pitcher?" Sterling asked.

"I'm glad he's on our side," Borden replied.

In the seventh inning, Trott Nixon broke up the no hitter with a checked-swing ground ball that A-Rod couldn't handle. Jethro didn't seem to care. He retired the rest of the side. By the eighth inning, his fastball was still clocking over one hundred and five.

The game ended with an exclamation point. Before going to the mound to start the ninth, Bodine and Posada were having a conversation in the Yankee dugout.

"I can't imagine what they could be discussing," John Sterling wondered, "unless they are late for dinner reservations after the game."

When he took the mound, Jethro quickly dispatched Renteria and Ortiz bringing Manny Ramirez to the plate. It was no secret that Jethro didn't like Ramirez. Manny had long scraggly hair and dressed out of sorts. Of all the players on both teams, he had been the most disrespectful towards the new pitcher, making hillbilly jokes and bragging about what he would do when he came to bat.

Jethro took a couple of extra seconds staring in at the plate before his first pitch, a strike on the inside corner. When he took the ball back from Posada, he paused to rub it up as he glared at the batter. Ramirez got good wood on the next pitch drilling it hard but foul down the left field line. Manny yelled something at the mound, and Jethro didn't seem amused. He wound up and threw a high, hard fastball, 'chin music' as they call it. Ramirez hit the deck to get out of the way.

"He isn't going to make any friends in this league doing that!" Susan Waldman exclaimed.

"I am glad that I don't have to bat against him," Sterling replied.

Terry Francona, the Red Sox manager, came running to the home plate umpire and started waving his hands.

"He can't do that. Throw him out of the game," he argued.

The home plate ump didn't much care for Manny Ramirez either and was secretly amused. He didn't eject anyone, but he did warn both managers. There were now two strikes and two outs. Jethro was one strike away from a first game, complete game, shutout victory. The fans were up on their feet. The pitcher peered in for a sign and again shook off his catcher.

"This is getting kind of old," Sterling sighed. "He shakes off every other pitch, but he hasn't thrown anything but a fastball all day."

Bodine wound up and threw. The ball started right for Ramirez's head. The batter hit the dirt, but then something strange happened. As the pitch was heading for the plate almost in slow motion, it started to bend, curving over the inside corner.

"Strike three!" the umpire shouted.

Manny got up and started dusting himself off. "You got to toss that kid," Manny told the umpire.

"Hard to toss him for throwing a strike," the ump replied.

I know, but that stuff is nasty. A guy could get hurt."

Jethro stole a quick look into the Red Sox dugout, tapped his spikes and walked off the mound.

"That boy won't need to be making moonshine if he can throw like that," was Sterling's last comment.

The next morning, the headlines of the New York Times read, "Kid from nowhere mows down the World Champion Red Sox."

That evening, on his show, The Apprentice, Donald Trump was lecturing the contestants as to why it was so hard to hit a four-seam fastball.

Chapter 4

Shea Stadium, two weeks later:

John Sterling had seen a lot in his seventeen years as the voice of the Yankees, but the last couple of days had been special. First, Terry Francona had held a press conference demanding that Jethro be given a steroid test, which he passed. It took a lot of convincing to get him to go into a bathroom stall with a test tube and a nebbish inspector who watched him pee. After the kid shut out Tampa Bay in his next start, Lou Pinella got into a shouting match with Jethro for throwing at Carl Crawford after a failed bunt attempt. Bud Selig asked to see the kid's birth certificate and wouldn't believe it when Brian Cashman told him that Pea Patch had lost all their birth records a few years ago in a Fourth of July fire. There was the obligatory cover story on Newsweek, and the National Enquirer claimed to have proof the Jethro was the love child of Elvis and an alien from outer space. Five days earlier, the kid had thrown another complete game shutout against the White Sox striking out eight of the last nine batters. The enthusiasm hadn't been lost on the rest of the team. The Yanks won eleven of twelve and were only two games out of first place. Without the pressure of being stoppers, Randy Johnson and Mike Mussina were pitching more effectively. With extra rest, Mariano Rivera and Flash Gordon were pitching like their old selves again.

Before every game, the media was all over Jethro. Brian Cashman assigned an intern to follow him and help with his interviews. In Cleveland, a reporter had asked Jethro if he was uncomfortable about anything in the Major Leagues.

"Hell," the kid answered back, "I get a little bored. I am used to pitching every day."

In the broadcast booth, John Sterling took note of the carnival atmosphere on the field. Shea Stadium was sold out for the first time that he could remember. There were more Yankee fans than Met fans in the seats. Outside, the scalpers were selling tickets at two hundred dollars each. Merchandisers had come up with souvenir balls painted with fiery comet tails. They were calling them "Jethroes."

The game got off to what was by then a normal start. The Yankees scored two in the second off a Hideki Matsui home run, and Jethro retired the side in order in both of the first two innings. Since the game was being played in a National League ballpark without a designated hitter, Jethro led off to start the Yankee third.

"It will be interesting to see what the kid can do with the bat, Susan," John Sterling said.

"Nothing that kid does surprises me anymore," Susan replied.

Pedro Martinez, the Mets' pitcher, started Jethro with a nasty slider that he took for strike one. He watched the next pitch, a fastball on the outer half of the plate, for strike two.

"It doesn't look like he is too anxious to swing," Sterling commented.

Susan started to say, "you don't have to bat when you can throw strikes over one hundred miles an hour," but before she could finish her sentence, Pedro threw another fastball over the meat of the plate. Jethro took a rip. For a second, the stadium went dead silent. Then, came a deafening roar. Usually, when a Yankee batter hits a homer, John Sterling yells, "that ball is high, it is far, it is gone!" but he said nothing as he watched the ball sail over the fence, over the stands and well into the parking lot.

After a few seconds of silence, Susan Waldman spoke first. "It would be doing an injustice to call that a long home run," was all she could think to say.

Jethro seemed a little embarrassed by all the commotion as he touched home and went back to the dugout. Even though he was on the visiting team, the fans yelled and screamed until he came out for a curtain call.

As the game progressed, the score was more of an afterthought. The Yanks scored in the fifth and three times in the seventh when Jethro tripled off the wall.

"He runs pretty fast, too," Sterling commented.

By the time he came to bat in the top of the ninth, Jethro had a home run, a double and a triple in his first three Major League at bats. The Yankees had a seven to nothing lead.

"Do you realize," Sterling said, "that young Mr. Bodine is one single away from becoming the first Yankee to hit for the cycle since Tony Fernandez did it eleven years ago?"

"Nothing that kid does surprises me," Susan replied for the third time that day.

The fans were into the game. Not one seat was empty even though the game was all but over.

Sensing the drama of the moment, Mets manager, Willie Randolph, brought in his closer, Bradon Looper, to face Jethro. Even though it was foolish to waste your closer in a game that couldn't be won, Randolph understood theatre. The first pitch was an inside fastball. Jethro turned on it and hit a screaming line drive down the left field line. The crowd groaned as the umpire called it foul. Looper wound up and pitched again, low and away. On the next pitch, Jethro squared and laid down a bunt. The third baseman was playing back and didn't have a chance as Jethro sprinted to first without a throw.

"So much for hitting the cycle," Susan Waldman said.

Derek Jeter was up next. He fouled off a pitch for a strike. Jethro was running, trying to steal second base. Joe Torre turned to Joe Girardi, his bench coach and told him to flash the 'don't run' signal.

"I didn't go over any signals with him," Girardi said.

"Why not?" Joe asked.

"I never thought he would get on base."

"Better send out a pinch runner then."

Tony Womack went out to replace Jethro. The kid came off the field to a thunderous ovation.

"Not a bad first three starts," Sterling announced, "three shutout victories, two complete games, hit for the cycle, and if the Red Sox lose today, the New York Yankees will be one game out of first place."

After the game, Jim Grey caught up with Jethro in the Yankee clubhouse.

"How come you never told us you could hit like that?"

"Shucks, nobody asked me," the kid replied.

"What kind of kool-aid do you guys drink in Pea Patch?" Grey asked trying to be funny.

"I don't know what you mean," Jethro answered.

"I mean I bet no one else in Pea Patch can hit the ball that far," Grey quipped as he started to move his microphone towards Gary Sheffield who was walking by.

"My brother, Abner, can."

Jim Grey wasn't sure he had heard correctly. "What did you just say kid?"

"I said my brother Abner hits the ball farther," Jethro answered very matter-of-factly.

"Why didn't he come to New York with you?" Grey asked, excited about the scoop he might have uncovered.

"Well you lamebrain," Jethro replied, "Abner is a better hitter and a pretty darn good center fielder, but everybody knows that the Yanks really needed a pitcher. Abner never was much of a pitcher."

Up in his box, George Steinbrenner was listening to the interview with George Bush Sr. The ex-president was in the midst of talking to the Yankee owner about some matters of national security.

"Excuse me, Mr. President," George said as he stepped into the hall feverishly punching numbers into his cell phone. "Cashman!" Steinbrenner yelled into the phone, " did you hear the interview? Get Abner Bodine on the phone and sign him to a contract."

"I heard it, too. I just tried to call, but there is no phone in the Bodine household," Cashman shouted back. He was running and out of breath. "I am on my way to the airport. Get hold of the pilot and have him get the plane ready. And George," Cashman caught his breath, "let's hope that Theo Epstein wasn't listening to the game."

Chapter 5

Pea Patch, West Virginia the next evening;

"Talk about the end of the road," Brian Cashman was thinking to himself. "I never would have got here without a little luck."

Brian had had quite a day. When he got to the airport to board the team jet, the pilot told him that he couldn't find Pea Patch on the map. No one at the FAA had a clue as to the location of the nearest airport. Cashman tried to call Jethro, but there was no answer. The internet was no help either. The only reference to Pea Patch was in a children's story. Cashman finally got hold of the club secretary of the Yank's AA affiliate in Wheeling, West Virginia. The secretary had never heard of Pea Patch either, but one of the players remembered that there used to be a town in the western part of the state that changed its name from Pea Patch to Century City when the town fathers wanted a more progressive image. Still, the nearest airport was 175 miles away. Upon arrival, the only car Brian could rent was an old Jeep with creaky windows and dusty seats. With a top speed of fifty miles per hour, the Yankees GM had to endure indignities of truck drivers blowing their horns and little old ladies giving him the finger as they passed him by. One hundred miles out of town, the pavement stopped, and Brian drove into the Appalachians on a narrow dirt road. He missed a turn in Shepherd, West Virginia only to drive twenty some miles before a jogger turned him around. He had a close call when his gas gauge started playing with empty. The nearest filling station was miles away. Luckily, he found a farmer that was happy to sell a stranger a tank of gas. After he filled up, the stranger priced the gas at ten dollars a gallon. Brian wasn't very happy, but it was a seller's market, and Brian was too tired to argue.

The faithful Yankees GM drove through the night. He might have stopped, but the motels he passed didn't look very sanitary. Most importantly, he didn't know where Theo Epstein, the Boston Red Sox general manager, might be.

By the next morning, Brian was getting discouraged. He had no idea where he was, and he wasn't getting any closer to Century City. He had a feeling that he was getting the run around from locals giving him misleading directions. The last person he talked to told him, "he couldn't get there from here, and that he would have to start from someplace else."

"Smart aleck," Brian thought to himself. Fortunately, he caught a lucky break. As dawn broke, blinded by the sun shining through the dust on his windshield, he pulled down his shade, put on his sunglasses and grabbed his Yankee cap out of his suitcase. As fate would have it, the next person he stopped for directions happened to be a Yankee fan.

"Do you know how to get to Pea Patch, young man? It might be known as Century City."

"Is that a real New York Yankees cap?" the young man replied.

"It is, and I am Brian Cashman, the Yankees GM. If you know how to get there, I can make it worth your while."

"Shit, everyone seems to be looking for Pea Patch. Another man just asked for directions a few minutes ago."

Brian started sweating.

"Can you help me get there?"

"Well, I might know a short cut. My name is Skeeter, and if you got two hundred dollars in your pocket, I'm your man."

"Hop in Skeeter," Brian said as he handed the boy a couple of one-hundred dollar bills.

Before starting his engine, Brian's cell phone rang. It was the Boss. "How is it going Brian, and where the hell are you? I have been trying to call you all day."

"No cell reception in the most of these parts, George. What can I do for you?"

"Well Brian, you better get your ass in gear. I called the Red Sox office, and Theo was out for the day. During the season, Theo never takes a day off."

"Take it easy, George. Skeeter and I will be there soon."

"Who is Skeeter?"

"Don't ask." Brian scraped the phone with his fingernail. "We're losing reception, George." He disconnected the phone. He was used to humoring Steinbrenner, but now he was real busy and real tired, and he wasn't in the mood.

"What about the other guy who asked for directions?" Brian asked Skeeter.

"Hell, he only gave me twenty bucks, and I sent him up the river," Skeeter replied.

Relieved, Brian turned the engine on. "Which way do we go?" he asked.

"If you're looking for the Bodine house, and I think you are," Skeeter snickered, "It's that one over there."

Sure enough, on the mail box across the street, in small green letters read the word, Bodine.

"Anything else I can do for ya?"

Cashman bit his tongue. "Thank you. I won't be needing your services any further." Brian knew he had been had, but he was energized by the thought that he was back on the hunt. He turned off onto a narrow road heading to the Bodine homestead. The scene was just as he had imagined. The road was littered with whiskey bottles and magazines. A couple of scraggly peach trees were on one side of the lane. As he approached an old clapboard house that needed a coat of paint, Brian spotted a make-shift baseball backstop off to the side. "I am the man," he thought to himself.

Brian parked in front of the house and started for the front door. As he approached, a couple of old bloodhounds came over and started sniffing him. The bigger of the two started to snarl. Brian was about to turn back when a lady's voice screamed, "What the hell you want, bud?"

"My name is Brian Cashman. I work for the New York Yankees, and I am looking for Abner Bodine."

The lady turned and looked behind the house. "Abner, you lazy rat, there's a Brian Cashman wants to see you. Says he's from the New York Yankees."

Abner Bodine was lying in a hammock between two shade trees, sucking a drink through a straw. When he heard the words, New York Yankees, he hopped out of the hammock and started running towards the house.

"Oh my God," Cashman thought to himself "that is one big kid."

The 'negotiations' were short and quick. Cashman was in no mood to wait for Theo Epstein to get there and complicate things. “We will give you fifty thousand for a five game trial, and if you make the team, as a bonus, we will build a nice house for your mom.” Cashman had done the arithmetic. A house might cost one hundred thousand dollars. Add that to the bonus and it was still only half of what the Yanks normally paid a mediocre high school prospect. If he could get Abner’s mark on the contract, Theo Epstein couldn’t even talk to him until after the season. By that time, Abner would be signed to a long-term deal, or he would be long gone.

Abner called his mother and brother into the kitchen. After about two minutes, he came out with a big smile of his face, “Mr. Cashman, sir, I’m your guy. Where do I sign?’ A stroke of the pen later, Abner Bodine was a New York Yankee.

“Get your stuff together, Abner. We are heading to New York.”

While Abner was packing, Cashman made the obligatory small talk with his folks. His mom was nice enough, but his brother, Hoss, “What a fat little turd,” Brian thought to himself. Hoss didn’t say two words the whole time he sat there, and whenever Brian talked to him, all he did was scratch himself and grin.

In any case, after two days on the chase, Brian Cashman had signed his player. With great relief, he started the car and headed out the driveway on his way back to the airport. The pilot would have the plane fueled and ready to fly back to New York in time for the start of a three game series against the Los Angeles Angels of Anaheim.

Chapter 6

When they landed in New York, Cashman and Abner headed directly to Yankee Stadium. Abner didn't talk much during the trip. After a while, the GM gave up trying to make conversation. Abner had never been on a plane before. When he got over the initial shock, he went over to the magazine rack in the cabin. "I should have brought some comic books," Cashman thought to himself. Abner picked out a Cosmopolitan. He thumbed through the pages quickly and then amused himself for the rest of the trip looking at the half-naked picture of Paris Hilton on the cover.

When they got to the ballpark, Joe Torre and Joe Girardi were waiting in the clubhouse. The plan was to hit some fungoes to Abner in centerfield and then throw some batting practice to see if he passed muster. Joe asked him a few questions before he took the field.

"You bat righty or lefty kid?"

"Mostly righty. I just bat lefty to screw around."

"How do you handle left handed pitchers?"

"Don't know. I never faced one."

"Can you lay down a sac bunt if I need you to?"

Abner thought about that one for a second. He grinned. "I don't think you will want me bunting, skipper."

Joe was going to ask a few more questions, but his intuition told him that this would be a good time to stop."See you on the field kid."

Girardi and Abner trotted out to shag some flies.

"I have got to make one call, and I'll be back," Torre said as he headed to his office. When Torre returned to the field a couple of minutes later, he had expected to see Abner in the outfield, but instead, the kid was sitting on the dugout steps.

"Well," asked Torre, expecting Girardi to tell him that the tryout was a farce.

The bench coach had an ashen look on his face. "All I have to say is," he paused to collect his words, "he's faster than Mantle, and," he paused again, "he's got the best arm that I have ever seen."

"Time for some batting practice," Torre said.

The Yanks had Randy Johnson and Mike Mussina, a lefty and a righty, standing by. Both of them were potential Hall of Fame pitchers. The way the schedule was set, this was their bullpen day. A little pitching wouldn't affect their next start. Girardi, a former catcher, went behind the plate. Don Mattingly, the batting coach, walked over to the cage to observe. Abner picked up a bat and dug in the box.

"Take it easy on the kid. He might be a little rusty," Mattingly hollered to the mound. Johnson went first. He was already warm, so batting practice was ready to begin. Abner took two of the ugliest practice swings that Torre had ever seen. Most Major Leaguers have what is known as a balanced swing. They take a short stride or no stride at all and finish in full control of their stance. When Abner swung, he had a high stride, more pronounced than Sadaharu Oh, the great Japanese slugger. The swing, neither fluid nor pretty, was so violent that Torre thought it might shatter glass. Mussina snickered to Johnson on the mound.

Abner watched the first pitch, a fastball right at the knees. He didn't swing at the next one either, a wicked curve that also dropped in for a strike.

"Take some cuts. He isn't trying to fool you," Mattingly said.

Abner swung at the next pitch, hitting a soft grounder, then a short pop fly. The next pitch was an easy line drive. Three of the next four went out of the park.

"Don't be easy on him," Mattingly shouted out to Randy.

"I'm not," Randy replied. The great left-hander was not amused. This was only batting practice, but Randy took it personally. Of course, the reason that he was a great pitcher was that he took everything personally.

"How's it going?" Mattingly asked Abner.

"I needed a couple to gauge the speed," Abner replied. "They're a little slower than I am used to."

"Good thing Randy didn't hear him say that," Mattingly whispered to Torre.

Mike Mussina took the mound next. The results were the same. After looking at a couple of off-speed pitches, Abner started drilling them in all directions.

"What do you think, skip?" Mattingly asked.

"I think we better call Cashman," Torre replied.

"Why's that?"

"Tell him to order a couple extra cases of baseballs for tonight's game." As he walked off the field, Joe's first thought was, "I wish Zimmer was here to see this."

Don Mattingly took Abner to the clubhouse to pick out his uniform. Sam Borden of the Daily News was waiting, having discovered this secret session.

"Donnie, what are you going to do to refine that swing?" he asked.

"Sam, what I am going to do is this," Mattingly replied. "When he comes up to bat, I am not going to say a thing. I am going to sit at the furthest end of the dugout, behind the biggest fence and hope he doesn't hit one at me."

Cletus was waiting for them in the equipment room. They picked out some spikes and a couple of fielding gloves. Abner didn't want any batting gloves. He took a couple swings with a few bats and liked the feel of the Gary Sheffield model. The cap presented a problem. They didn't have one quite big enough. Cletus fixed that by cutting a little piece out of the band. One of the standing jokes in baseball lore was about the big kid from nowhere that comes into the equipment room, needing an extra large everything except for a small jock, but Abner needed a big one of those, also. They were just about done when Cletus asked Abner what number he would like.

"I'll take number three," Abner declared. The room became silent.

Brian Cashman was in George Steinbrenner's office bragging about his conquest. Rudy Giuliani was with them delighting in every detail of the trip. They had watched Abner's batting practice. George was fantasizing about the 'Owner of the Year' speech that he would probably be giving. Cashman was telling George that he was going to charge the team for a new pair of shoes if he couldn't get the manure off his loafers. The phone rang.

"I thought I said no calls!" Steinbrenner yelled to his secretary.

"Joe Torre is on the line, and he says it is urgent."

The Boss put the call on speaker. "Yes, Joe."

"Mr. Steinbrenner, Abner won't play unless he can wear number three."

Anyone who knows anything about the history of the New York Yankees, or anyone who knows anything about baseball knows that the great Babe Ruth wore number three. The number was retired with him, never to be seen in pinstripes again. It was enshrined in Monument Park behind center field with the other Yankee greats, Gehrig, DiMaggio, Mantle, etc.

"Well, give him a cookie and tell him to wear thirty-three," George yelled, annoyed that he should be bothered with this type of problem.

"Won't work, George. He says three is the only number that he ever wore and that if he can't wear it, he is going home. We talked to Jethro, and he says that when Abner gets stubborn, nothing can change his mind."

"Did you tell him that three was the Babe's number?"

"He asked us why Babe needed the number if he was dead."

"Keep him in the clubhouse, Joe. We'll come up with something." George hung up the phone. The Boss had a dilemma. If he gave in and let Abner wear three, the New York establishment would crucify him. If he sent Abner home, he might lose the pennant and the accolades that go with it, not to mention the money. When Yogi Berra had left the Yankees in a huff, George had eaten crow. He traveled to see Yogi with his hat in his hand. He had taken one for the team, but this was different. This was number three of Yankee legends. This was the Babe.

Brian Cashman spoke first. "We can't do it, George. It would cause a mutiny. There would be blood in the streets."

"Cashman," there was wrath in the Boss' tone, "I don't pay you to tell me the problem. I pay you to find the answers."

Rudy Giuliani had been silent, in deep thought, but now he spoke, "Gentlemen, I might have an idea. Suppose..."

Chapter 7

They say that in the Wild West, newspapers would separate fact from legend and print the legend. In the Bronx, baseball owners weigh principle against winning pennants and opt to win pennants. The Yankees' brain trust deliberated and came up with a unique solution. Drawing on the pragmatism from years of dealing with diverse interests of the Big Apple, Rudy Giuliani outlined his plan.

"What we have here is a simple but well framed problem. On the one hand, we have the Babe, a loveable icon immortalized in Monument Park, but like Abner said, he is dead, and he can't play center field. On the other hand, we have a big, strong centerfielder with a rifle arm, speed and power. This is a no-brainer. We just have to find a way to sell it to the public."

"That shouldn't be too hard," George piped in. "New Yorkers will buy anything that helps us win ball games."

"We don't have time to dance around," Cashman cautioned. "Game time is only three hours away."

There was a short silence. Rudy continued, "The Babe was an orphan. What if in this terrible year of war and strife, the New York Yankees pay tribute to all the orphans in the world? What if the New York Yankees find an orphan to honor the Babe's memory by playing center field and wearing his number three?"

"That's a little bit of a stretch isn't it?" Brian asked.

But now Rudy was on a roll, "The hurricanes, the earthquake, the war in Iraq have all left poor orphans hungry and freezing. The Yankees have to do their part to draw attention to their pain and suffering."

"That's such crap, Rudy," Brian said.

The Boss cut Brian off. "We all know its crap, Cashman. The only question is is there a market for it, and I believe there is."

Cashman spoke again. "I see one big problem that you are both missing. Abner and Jethro are not orphans."

"Yeah," said Steinbrenner, "but they could be."

Brian thought for a moment. "You might have something there. Based on the advanced state of record keeping in Pea Patch, I doubt that anyone could say if their momma really is their momma." There was a twinkle in the GM's eye. "I bet for a new refrigerator, their momma might even forget."

"I have another thought," the Mayor exclaimed. "What if we honored one of the Babe's descendants by having him throw out the first pitch on Orphan's Day?"

"Brilliant!" the Boss exclaimed. "You see, Cashman, that's how a pro makes small problems go away."

With the solution in hand, they scurried off to execute their plan. Game time was approaching. It turned out that finding one of the Babe's descendants was more challenging than anyone had imagined. The Babe was a prolific character and over the years had spread his seed in many different directions. Dozens of illegitimate offspring roamed the city proudly claiming that Babe Ruth was their father or grandfather. Finding the proper heir to carry the go along with the ruse was even more difficult as most of the Babe's known heirs were unwilling to cooperate. Again, Rudy Giuliani was up to the task.

Sal Maclone, the police chief of New York City, was still a good friend. Rudy explained the urgency of the problem and asked him if he could deploy the department's resources to find a willing heir. The chief's first reaction was that it would be a violation of civil liberties to track someone without due cause. However, after a brief discussion and suggestion of seats behind home plate through the playoffs, the chief rationalized that the morale of the city would be lifted by such a symbolic act. After all, a proactive police department needed to recognize that improved morale might lower the crime rate. Furthermore, Maclone could use the publicity if he went through with his plans to run for district attorney.

After a couple of hours of intense detective work, Claire Ruth Martinez Markowitz was found in Queens, NY where she was finishing her shift as a maid in the Long Island City Holiday Inn. Claire was indeed a great granddaughter of George Herman "Babe" Ruth.

"After all these years, why do you want me to throw out the first pitch?" she asked skeptically.

It didn't take long to convince her. A limo ride to the ballpark, the promise of a couple of new outfits, a few bucks and a case of Scotch did the trick. That night, the Boss came onto the field and introduced her to the crowd. There were tears in his eyes as he said, "The legacy of the Babe represents hope for all the poor and underprivileged youth in the world. The New York Yankees take pride in asking all New Yorkers and baseball fans to do their part to ease the suffering of those less fortunate. It is with great pride that we have asked Abner Bodine, an orphan in his own right, to help us pay tribute to this noble cause by wearing the number three, worn by the greatest Yankee of them all,

Babe Ruth. Babe grew up an orphan in the streets of Baltimore before coming to New York. I am proud to introduce Claire Ruth Martinez Markowitz, the Babe's great-granddaughter, to throw out the first pitch." As Claire approached the mound, a weekday sellout crowd, stood and cheered.

The game was anticlimactic. Abner played center and batted third. Jethro, on a day off from pitching, was the DH and batted fourth. The fans bought into the charade and gave the 'orphans' a standing ovation at every opportunity. The Yanks won the game easily, and the fans got their money's worth. Abner struck out in his first at bat but ended up three for five with a double and a monstrous home run. Jethro had a couple of doubles, two runs scored and a walk. The plays of the game took place in the Angels' half of the fifth inning. With Chone Figgins on second and no outs, Vlad Guerrero hit a high fly that looked like it would clear the center field fence. Running at full speed, Abner hit the wall and jumped several feet into the air to snag the ball.

"Never seen a catch like that!" John Sterling exclaimed.

"There has been a lot of stuff we haven't seen this year," Susan Waldman chipped in.

"What do you think about that, Sam?" Sterling asked Sam Borden who again was in the booth for the Daily News Fifth.

"Thank God those boys are on our side," was Borden's standard reply.

As spectacular as the catch was, the next play was even better. Chone Figgins had taken third tagging up on the last play. With one out, Garrett Anderson came to bat. On Shawn Chacon's third pitch, he hit a fly ball to deep center. Chone Figgins, the fastest runner in the American League tagged up at third.

"Figgins will score easily," Sterling announced. "Too bad, because we heard that Abner has a strong arm. He wouldn't have a chance at a slow runner from that deep."

But in what was becoming a fairy tale season, another chapter was about to be written. Abner caught the ball on the warning track. In one continuous motion, he uncorked a bullet throw to the plate.

"He's coming home!" Sterling shouted, "and here comes the throw."

The screams in the Ballpark drowned out the announcers call. Then a second later, "He's out! I don't believe what I just saw with my own eyes. He's out!" There was no comment from Susan Waldman, but a loud clank came over the airwaves. She had dropped her microphone.

The final score was ten to three. With the Red Sox losing, the Yanks had taken first place. After the game, there were several interesting interviews. Sal Maclone talked about the message that the Yankees had sent to the poor kids of the city. He added that the current district attorney of New York could learn a lot from the example. Joe Torre said that using Jethro as his DH would help him rest his veterans down the stretch. However, Abner's interview gave the press their best copy.

Jim Grey asked him about his catch and throw. Abner didn't have much comment. His next question was, "I bet you boys would argue about who batted clean up for your team back in Pea Patch?"

"Hell, it wasn't much of a contest."

"What do you mean?" Grey queried. "Was it you or Jethro?"

"Neither one."

"What do you mean?" Grey pressed.

"Neither of us had half the stick of our brother Hoss."

After a moment of silence, "Let's go back upstairs to the booth," was all that Jim Grey could think to say.

In their box, Steinbrenner and Cashman were celebrating the victory with Donald Trump and Rudy Giuliani when they heard Abner's comment. "Damn," said Cashman, "I wouldn't have guessed that fat little turd brother of theirs could get off the couch much less play ball."

"Cancel your dinner reservation. You will be flying back to Pea Patch tonight," the Boss ordered.

"Before you come back this time," Rudy said, "maybe you should ask him if they have any more brothers or cousins." Everybody laughed.

"Wait a minute," The Donald added. "Maybe you should also ask if there are any sisters or aunts." Everyone nodded.

Chapter 8

The next morning, Brian Cashman drove up the Bodine driveway for a second time. Instead of the broken down jeep from his last trip, he was behind the wheel of a brand new Hummer. His plan was to leave the car at the Century City Airstrip. With all the cash flow the Bodine boys had created, the Hummer was money well spent. He figured he might be making several more trips to Pea Patch over the next few years. Ma Bodine must have known that he was coming. She was waiting for him at the door.

"Amazing how fast news travels," Cashman thought to himself, "especially without phone service."

"Why Mr. Cashman, nice to see you again. You are just in time for breakfast."

"Good Morning, Mrs. Bodine."

"Oh call me Daisy," Mrs. Bodine blushed.

Brian looked at his watch. Eleven-thirty seemed like a late hour to eat breakfast, but he had been traveling all night, and he was hungry. He took another look at Mrs. Bodine. She was a big woman probably in her late forties. She was somewhat attractive, but it was easy to tell that she had been worked hard. Her arms were well muscled, and her face noticeably wrinkled for a woman of her age. Today, she was wearing what looked to be an old prom dress. Apparently, she wanted to present well for her gentleman caller.

As Cashman entered the living room, he noticed that Hoss hadn't moved from his last visit a couple of days ago. He was sitting in the same chair sipping from the same cup. Hoss didn't look anything like a ballplayer. Small and pudgy, he looked more like a butterball turkey with short arms and legs sticking out. His hair was crew cut. "I hope this isn't some kind of joke," the GM thought to himself.

"How are you doing, kid?" Brian asked. Hoss didn't answer. He just grinned. "How would you like to come to New York and play some ball in Yankee Stadium?"

Hoss grinned again. Cashman reluctantly forced his next comment, "The Yankees need you to play ball with your brothers."

Daisy came to the rescue. "Hoss doesn't talk much, but he misses his brothers. His feelings were hurt when you signed Abner instead of him, he being the better hitter."

"What positions can he play?"

Hoss grinned again, and his mother answered. "Hoss is a little slow to play the field. He used to play first, but not very well. Jethro wrote and told us that the Yankees use a designated hitter. That might be right up Hoss' alley."

"I can give you the same five-game contract that I gave Abner."

"We can talk business after we eat," Daisy said.

Breakfast was a little awkward. Hoss didn't talk, and Brian had the uncomfortable feeling that Mrs. Bodine might be coming on to him. After coffee, he decided to ask where Mr. Bodine might be.

"We haven't heard from that SOB in years."

Cashman thought he saw Hoss chuckle. After they were finished eating, the GM pulled out the contract. "I need some information young man." Cashman asked the standard questions, birth date, social security number, medical history, etc. For every answer, Hoss grinned while Daisy provided the information.

'What's your proper legal name to appear on the contract?"

"Eugene," Daisy answered.

"Why do they call you Hoss?" Hoss started to blush, the first reaction that Cashman had seen in over three hours.

"No good reason," Daisy answered quickly.

Brian changed the subject, and after a little small talk, the contract was signed.

Hoss grabbed his duffel, which was already packed, took his bat and glove off the shelf and headed out to the Hummer with the general manager. "I hope you will come to New York to see your sons play," Brian said as he sat behind the wheel.

"Oh, I would love to," Daisy replied in the sweetest voice she could muster. With that, the GM and his new prospect headed back to the Bronx.

Yankee Stadium later that day:

George Steinbrenner was looking at Hoss' picture on the front page of the Daily News. When Cashman came into the office, he had a big smile on his face. The Boss showed him the newspaper. "This is the best PR we've had in years. We don't have a single ticket left to sell this season."

"Hoss wants to wear number five," Cashman said. "That was Joe DiMaggio's number."

The Boss wasn't even fazed. "No problem, Brian," he responded, "Hoss can wear number five as a tribute to his Italian heritage."

"Hoss Bodine of Italian heritage," Brian muttered with an incredulous look on his face.

“We’re winning games,” the Boss’s replied. “If the people even notice that, then we have a problem. Just get him ready for Clemens’ fastball.”

The Houston Astros were in town for an inter league game. Roger Clemens was pitching. Steinbrenner had never forgiven the ‘Rocket’ for leaving the Yankees two years earlier to play in Houston, his hometown. Tonight, George was looking forward to revenge. The Rocket would have to pitch against the Bodine boys.

When Joe Torre asked the boys how they felt about facing Roger Clemens, Abner asked him, “Roger who.” A reporter for the Post overheard the remark. He had just enough time to make “ROGER WHO?” the headline for the afternoon addition. The first question Clemens was asked when he got to the ballpark was if he had seen the headline. He gave a short and explicit answer. Apparently, the future Hall of Famer had seen the paper, and he wasn’t amused.

Chapter 9

Cletus had a tough time fitting Hoss with his uniform for the opposite reasons as with Jethro and Abner. While his brothers were tall, sleek, athletic and sculpted, Hoss was short and fat, Yogi Berra with twice the gut. Joe DiMaggio, The Yankee Clipper, would have rolled over in his grave if he saw number five on this one, Cletus thought to himself.

Randy Johnson was on the mound for the Yanks pitching against Clemens. Normally that would have been the story, two Hall of Famers toe to toe in the Bronx, but today it was just a byline to the Bodine boys versus the Rocket. In the pregame manager's show, Joe Torre said he hoped Roger wouldn't throw the fastball high and tight, as was his tendency when he was mad. He also said that Randy Johnson, who was intimidated by no one, would do whatever was necessary to protect his players.

The game started out as a pitchers duel. Both the Big Unit and the Rocket brought their A game. Through eight innings, the score was zero to zero. Both teams had managed only four hits. Abner had a blooper to center in the fourth inning. He was the Yanks' only threat to score after stealing second and third, but was stranded when Giambi struck out. Hoss was the bigger story going one for three. He hit two long fly balls that went foul by inches. His hit was a single off the center field wall. A faster runner might have made it to third base. "I wonder if that's why they call him Hoss?" John Sterling commented from the press box. "I bet he hits mostly singles and home runs."

"He's no Carl Crawford," Susan Waldman replied.

The announcers had noticed an interesting side note about the new slugger. Before each of his at bats, he went to a corner of the dugout. Facing the wall away from the television cameras, he went through a series of isometrics.

"You'll have to ask him about that in the club house report, Susan."

"It will be my first question," Susan responded.

By the ninth inning, both hurlers had thrown over one hundred pitches. There was no one up in either bullpen.

"A team of horses couldn't get Randy or Roger out of this game," Sterling said. "Pitch counts mean nothing now. This is mano-a-mano."

Randy gutted his way through the top of the ninth. Craig Biggio doubled to open the inning and was sacrificed to third. Randy walked Berkman and Saunders to load the bases, but then struck out Ausmus and Taveras to retire the side.

In the bottom of the ninth, the Yankees had Robinson Cano, Abner and Hoss due up. As the home team came off the field, the fans started cheering. In the dugout, Jethro Bodine was grabbing a bat.

"Roger who, Roger who," it was so deafening that John Sterling could hardly hear himself over the roar of the crowd. "I don't know if anyone can hear me," Sterling shouted into the mike, "but it's the ninth inning. The Rocket, the best pitcher of our generation, facing three Bodine boys in a scoreless game. This game could end on any pitch. It doesn't get any better than this!"

The first pitch to Jethro was a bullet under the chin that knocked the big rookie down. "He'll have to be careful," Susan Waldman exclaimed. "If he hits Jethro or Abner with their speed, he could end up with the winning run on second or third with less than two outs. If he hits Hoss, we'll see Tony Womack pinch-running for sure."

"Roger won't hit anyone," Sterling replied. "He knows exactly what he's doing. He's been doing it for years."

On the second pitch, Jethro laid down a bunt, and it was a beauty. Clemens came off the mound hard, but didn't have a play.

"They weren't expecting that," Sterling said. "The plot thickens."

"No pitcher likes to be bunted on, especially in a situation like this," Susan said. "Clemens doesn't look amused."

"He's got to keep an eye on the runner. It's hard enough to pitch to Abner without any distractions."

Predictably, the first pitch to Abner was high and tight, and like his brother before him, Abner hit the deck. Torre started to come out of the dugout, but Abner waved him back. The noise in the stands went up several decibels.

"I wonder why the umps don't give him a warning?" Susan mused.

"Twenty plus years in the big leagues gives him a license," Sterling replied. "Besides, the Bodines are rookies who talk a lot. The umps are going to give the Rocket some room."

On the next pitch, Jethro broke for second. Abner stepped into an inside fastball and got hit on the shoulder. The trainer ran out, but Abner brushed it off and headed to first. There were two runners on and no outs.

The noise level went up again. Hoss was sauntering up to the plate. As he dug in, Roger glared at the batter. Hoss grinned and tapped his bat on the plate. The first pitch was a nasty splitter. Hoss swung and missed it by a mile.

"Welcome to the big leagues," Sterling commented. "He'll see that one again."

"He should get something to hit," Susan said. "Roger can't walk the winning run to third with no outs."

"He can't hit him either," Sterling replied. "That takes away the inside part of the plate."

The second pitch was a fastball, belt high, just off the plate. Hoss swung and hit a bullet.

"If it stays fair," Sterling shouted. "It's a...foul ball, just missed. A couple of inches and this one would have been in the books. Hoss is down 0-2 in the count. That makes the splitter more effective. Roger sets for the next pitch, and here it comes, and it's a hard drive down the line, what a bullet. This one is high. It is far, and...it's off the foul pole, a three-run walk off home run. The ball game is over. Theeeeeeeeeeee Yankees winnnnnnnnnnnnnnn. This is a win for the ages."

As Frank Sinatra crooned New York, New York, Hoss started to round the bases.

"They might have to play it again, by the time he rounds second," Susan said. "Anyway, I am heading down to the clubhouse."

The Rocket was walking off the field with a scowl on his face. In the Yankees' dugout, Randy Johnson was nodding his head. Hoss finally got to home plate and grinned as he was mobbed by his teammates.

On the replay, John Sterling had two comments. The first was that the pitch Hoss hit was another splitter, and a good one. The second comment was in his own words, "I think the foul pole is leaning. I'm not kidding. I think Hoss broke the foul pole."

Down on the field, Susan Waldman wasted no time in finding the hero of the game. Abner came over to interpret. "Tell me about the last pitch. Our friends in the booth say it was another splitter. You really looked bad on the first one."

"Hoss threw him a bone," Abner replied for his brother.

"Tell me about those exercises you do in the dugout before you bat."

Hoss grinned. Neither of the brothers said anything.

"One last question. Why do they call you Hoss?"

Again, Hoss started to blush. "No good reason," Abner answered for his brother with an uncomfortable look on his face. Just then, one of the mounted police on the field rode by. All of a sudden, Hoss' face lit up with a big smile. He started to walk towards the animal. Abner quickly stepped in his way. "Time to head to the clubhouse," he said. The interview was over.

Chapter 10

The day had started well for George Steinbrenner. The surging Yankees were in first place by three games. The players were performing with confidence, producing at their highest levels. The Bodine boys were knocking the stitches off the ball. Every fifth day, Jethro was unhittable on the mound. Even role players like Bubba Crosby and John Flatery were rising to the occasion. Opposing pitchers, scared of putting runners on base in front of the Bodines, were giving the rest of the team better pitches to hit. A-Rod was pounding home runs. Sheffield's and Jeter's batting averages were up over 30 points each. The fans were pouring money into the team's coffers like never before. Every game was a sellout. Subscriptions to the YES cable network were growing ten percent every week. The team was on track to earn upwards of $300 million for the year.

"Eat your heart out, Boston," Steinbrenner thought to himself. "We'll have some fun when David Ortiz and Jason Varitek become free agents next year."

The boss even hired a PR firm solely to promote the Bodines. Rubicam and Young made sure that billboards all over the city had their pictures promoting everything from rental cars to ice cream. Yankees jerseys with the numbers three, four and five were hot items in every store (Jethro started wearing number four to show solidarity with Lou Gehrig and victims of ALS and other debilitating diseases). Souvenir stands in the stadium were peddling hillbilly hats with the team logo. The concession stands were selling 'moonshine' and 'possum dogs' instead of lemonade and franks.

Nevertheless, things were about to change. A famous westerner once said, "Nirvana is fleeting. When everything is going well, destiny creates a giant vacuum that sucks problems out of nowhere."

The Boss was looking at his schedule, a morning interview with the Daily News, afternoon meetings to sign the Bodine boys to multi-year contracts, a press conference afterwards to announce the signings. Late afternoon, he would film an episode of The Apprentice, in which he and The Donald would lecture candidates about success, hard work and ethical practices.

The phone rang. It was Brian Cashman. "George, we're all set for two o'clock."

"Good job, Bri boy." He called him 'Bri boy' when he was in a good mood even though he knew that the GM hated it.

"I told them to bring an agent just like you said."

"Good," the Boss replied. "We wouldn't want to look like we were taking advantage of such fine young citizens."

"That don't read, write or talk too well for that matter," Cashman completed the Boss' sentence.

"Who are they bringing?"

"I don't know, but what does it matter. They can't sign with anyone else this late in the season, and whatever they get is more than they could earn working in Pea Patch for a lifetime. Besides, we can throw them a bone. Maybe, we should build a modern ball field in Pea Patch in their honor."

George liked the sound of this tactic. "See you a little before two. Keep up the good work, Bri." George hung up and called his secretary, "Get my barber over here this morning. I need to look good for the press conference."

The morning went quickly. There were countless calls from well-wishers, Governor Pataki, Spike Lee and even President Bush. All had the same content. "Congratulations on your season. Is there anything I can do to help? Oh by the way, could you spare some tickets for tonight's game?" The calls were mildly bothersome, but the Boss loved the spotlight. As long as the team was winning and the Bodines were delighting the fans, the Yankees were the big ticket in town. In times like these, George could phone any CEO, and they would interrupt their board meetings to take his call. When the team was losing in years past, he would call his mother and it might take two weeks for her to phone him back.

Finally, two o'clock arrived. Brian and George were sitting in the conference room waiting when George's secretary, Mary, spoke over the intercom, "Sorry to interrupt you, Mr. Steinbrenner, but the Reverend Sharpton is here to see you."

"Shit," the boss replied, "not now. Tell him some other time. We're just about to meet with the boys and their agent."

"Sorry, Mr. Steinbrenner," Mary said in a low weak voice, "The Reverend Sharpton is here with the Bodines. He says he is their agent."

The boss looked at his GM, "What the fuck have we got ourselves into now?"

Then after taking a deep breath to compose himself, "Mary, please show the Reverend and his clients in."

Chapter 11

Al Sharpton and his 'clients' walked in like a mother duck with three ducklings in single file behind. The Reverend was wearing a loud, orange suit with an explosively bright tie. The Bodine boys were wearing cheap suits they had bought at Wal-Mart just for the occasion. They looked out of place and uncomfortable, especially Hoss, whose suit was about two sizes too big. After they were seated, George spoke first.

"Nice to see you again, Reverend."

"Cut the crap, George. You are never happy to see me."

Brian turned to the ball players, "Reverend Sharpton is an odd choice for an agent. How did you happen to pick him?"

Abner answered, "The Reverend went down to see Mama, and they seemed to hit it off well. She made us promise to trust him."

"Crafty bastard," George thought to himself.

Brian Cashman's mind was elsewhere. He remembered how Daisy seemed to be coming on to him, and the thought of Daisy and the Reverend; He decided he didn't want to go there.

"What can you offer for the services of these fine young men?"

The GM looked around the room before answering. Jethro was picking his teeth. Abner was scratching himself, and Hoss was squirming in his chair. "I went to Harvard Business School for this?" he thought to himself.

"We recognize that these boys have made a positive impact on this team. I'm hoping that we can wrap this up quickly. We are in a pennant race and with things going well, we don't want any distractions. We are willing to make the Bodines very comfortable."

"I know all about the pennant race," Sharpton replied. "Let's have a number."

"We were thinking about five million each for a five year contract. One million per year is a lot of money for rookies. It's more than they would make in Pea Patch in a lifetime."

Al Sharpton was many things, but a shrinking violet was not one of them. "Let's go boys," he said. They all got up and started to leave.

"Whoa now, Reverend," the Boss broke in. "What did you have in mind?"

"Mr. Steinbrenner," Sharpton stood up and started speaking as if from the pulpit, "we have a full agenda, but before we even get to the terms and conditions, we've got to agree on money. One million per year isn't even in the ballpark. Do these boys look like slaves to you? Are you running a cotton plantation?"

Cashman could see Sharpton was gaining momentum and decided to cut him short. "What did you have in mind? Remember, we are already paying luxury tax this year."

"I know how much the boys are making you. A-Rod makes $20 million per year. I realize the boys haven't been around as long as he has. They will settle for $17 million each per year, and they want ten years *guaranteed*."

The Boss' face got red. "That's five hundred and ten million. That would be a quarter of the team's total payroll. That's more than I make. I wouldn't pay the pope that much. Get your stinking butt out of my office."

George Steinbrenner was used to having his way, but with Al Sharpton, he had met his match. “My clients will not be playing this evening or any other evening until this matter is settled. You know how to reach me.” Sharpton knew he had the upper hand, and he was loving it. “Let’s go boys,” he said, and the four of them left the room.

Steinbrenner and Cashman sat for a minute, stunned. Finally, George spoke. “You had to tell them to get an agent,” he said, forgetting that was his idea to begin with. He hit a button on his intercom. “Cancel my appointments for the rest of the day.” He looked at his watch. “Send the jet down to Columbus. We still have time to get Crosby and Phillips to town for tonight’s game. Hell, we can beat Kansas City without the Bodines. If Sharpton wants to play dirty, he can bring it on. He’s not pushing me around. Cashman, speak to the Bodines directly and see if you can talk some sense into them. Pay them off. Do whatever you have to do. Get them to change their agent.”

Cashman sat quietly. Finally, George asked him, “Well, what’s your take?”

“I think we might have a problem. If we don’t sign those boys, we don’t have the horses to go all the way, and even worse, the press will eat us alive. I need to think.”

“Well, think on your own time. Your job is to make this go away, and game time is approaching. Let Torre know he’s got to make some changes to his lineup.”

CHAPTER 12

Cashman and Steinbrenner sat in their skybox with ashen faces. It was the seventh inning, and the Yanks were losing to Kansas City twelve to two. To say the game was a disaster would have been an understatement. The loss of the Bodine boys had had a demoralizing effect in the clubhouse.

Al Sharpton had been busy. There was a well-organized rally outside the front gate. Fans held signs reading "Trade George," "I love you Hoss," and "The Yankees, just say No." Leaders from the major labor unions in town were passing out leaflets demanding fair treatment for the young men from Pea Patch. Radio stations were extolling fans to turn in their tickets and boycott the team. The Reverend was holding a press conference vilifying the Yankees for a century long tradition of exploiting the poor and the weak. "The time had come," he screamed "to stand up to Mammon." The paid attendance of twenty-eight thousand was the lowest in years.

Cashman knew better than to say anything. The Boss kept looking back and forth between action on the field and a television interview being conducted with Sharpton on the street. Donald Trump, whose image prohibited him from association with any losing effort, had left the box after the third inning. In the fourth inning, Bubba Crosby, standing in for Abner in centerfield made a spectacular diving catch, yet the fans booed. In the sixth, Andy Phillips, the other replacement, hit a home run and was rewarded with boos once again. Yankee fans were always vocal, and they loved controversy. They were going to make sure management knew exactly how they felt.

"This is such crap, Brian. After all I have done for this team and this city. Sharpton is covering us with crap," George lamented

"Everyone knows its crap, George, but there is a real market for it," Cashman replied, secretly delighted that he could throw the analogy back at his employer.

Events on the field continued to deteriorate. By the ninth inning, the Yankees had gone through their whole bullpen and had to bring Mariano in to mop up. With his usual efficiency, Mariano dispatched the Royals one, two, three. As he walked off the field, the usually composed and gentlemanly reliever made a gesture directed at the owner's box, an action that was not missed by the Yankees' radio team.

"Mariano isn't very happy," John Sterling commented. "I don't think I have ever seen Mariano that upset before."

"Mariano isn't the only one," Susan Waldman replied.

When the microphones were off during a commercial, Sterling whispered, "We just lost by thirteen runs to Kansas City. Can you believe it? We got beat by a fucking AAA team, a bunch of minor leaguers."

"If that asshole wants a fight, he is going to get one," were Steinbrenner's last words for the evening. "The agent's share of a five hundred and ten million dollar contract would be fifty one million. I will sell the team before I give him that type of money."

The next morning, the front page of the Daily News had a picture of Al Sharpton sitting by the phone. The caption read, "Waiting for the Boss to call."

As bad as the first game of the series was, the second game was even worse. The Yanks activated Kevin Brown to take Jethro's start. Kevin, a top pitcher in his time, was battling a chronically bad back. Pitching in pain, Kevin gave up two runs before he got the first out. By the time the inning was over, the Bombers were trailing by six. By the third inning, when a slow drizzle started to fall, many of the crowd of fifteen thousand that braved the Reverend's boycott and the bad weather headed for the exits. There was a bigger crowd on the streets where Hillary Clinton joined Al Sharpton leading a rally. Arlo Guthrie and Joan Baez sung to the crowd, and the teamsters passed out beer and chips. The noise from the street drowned out Bob Sheppard, the stadium PA announcer.

"George won't be selling many franks or peanuts tonight," Sterling said.

The players were not pleased either. The Bodine boys were their ticket to the postseason. With yesterday's loss and the Red Sox victory, The Yankees had fallen back to a tie for the lead. The Sox had already won that afternoon. Tonight's pending loss was going to put the Yanks into second place. In the third inning, Derek Jeter tweaked an ankle sliding into second and asked to come out of the game.

"I have never seen Derek want to come out of a game in ten years. I didn't think a heart attack would sideline him," Waldman mused.

At the end of the fourth inning, Hideki Matsui headed off the field and back to the clubhouse. He didn't appear in the rest of the contest. After the game, he said through an interpreter that he felt nauseous and it might be time to end his twelve-year streak of consecutive games.

"What will happen next?" Sterling asked.

"Your guess is as good as mine," Waldman replied.

When he left his box at the end of the game, George Steinbrenner was not quite as combative as he was the day before. “We had better talk to Sharpton. Take your hat in your hand,” he instructed his general manager.

The next day, the front page of the Daily News had two pictures next to each other. The first was a photo of Daisy Bodine standing in front of her shack in a tattered dress on a snowy day. The caption read, “Trying to stay warm.” The second photo showed Steinbrenner and Trump in tuxedos smoking cigars in the Rainbow Room overlooking Rockefeller Plaza. The caption said, “Spending their millions.”

Cashman and Sharpton met for a bargaining session the next afternoon at Sharpton’s office in his Harlem church. “Can’t we sort this out at the end of the season?” Cashman asked. “If the players come back now, you have my word that I will give you my full attention and make a fair offer.”

“Righteousness waits for no one,” was Sharpton’s reply.

Cashman knew he was in a corner, and he knew that with the election coming up in November and Sharpton running for mayor, the Reverend wanted the spotlight now.

“How about two million each for the rest of this season, and we hammer out a longer contract this winter?”

“Good luck with KC tonight,” was Sharpton’s reply. “Do I need to bring my broom?”

“I’ll show myself out,” the GM said as he headed to the door.

The third game of the series was the low point of season. It might have been the low point of the last twenty years. Gary Sheffield, Jorge Posada and Jason Giambi had to miss the game with the flu. Mike Mussina served up three home run balls in the first inning. Attendance was less than five thousand, many of whom had been issued free passes. The YES network, which broadcast the Yankee games on cable, was short of advertisers. Outside the stadium, the mob was growing. Fans were burning the Boss in effigy and the NYPD was urging people to keep their kids away. At his daily press briefing, the Reverend Sharpton was telling everyone to stay calm and asking people to pray for Abner, Hoss, Jethro, Brian and George. "The Lord is vengeful, but he is just. His will is hard to understand, but his will be done."

Kansas City won the game eighteen to nothing and swept the series. By the last inning, there were more stadium workers in the building than fans. The Bombers were two games out of first.

On a preview of his evening talk show, Larry King announced that he was going to interview a 'reliable' source that claimed to have knowledge exposing George Steinbrenner of tax evasion. The Boss had met his match.

At three in the morning, the phone rang in Cashman's hotel room. Cashman knew who it was before he answered it. "Hello, George," he said in a sleepy voice.

"Brian, I want to meet with the boys' agent at eight o'clock tomorrow morning, and I want you over here now!"

Chapter 13

By the time Al Sharpton arrived at Yankee Stadium at nine in the morning, Brian Cashman had put in a full day. The Boss had reminded him repeatedly that he had created the problem by telling the boys to get an agent and since it was his problem, he had better fix it. They had discussed various strategies and tactics, but had not come up with a silver bullet. Al Sharpton showed up an hour late for the meeting. He had a Starbucks Latte in one hand and a greasy doughnut in the other. He watched George grimace as he laid the doughnut on the brightly polished furniture. He loved dealing from a position of strength. He knew he held all the aces.

"Tough luck in yesterday's game," The Reverend said with a straight face as he bit into his doughnut. "Mussina just didn't have it. You'll have better luck tonight against the Cardinals."

"Thanks for your warm words Al," Cashman said. "How are we going to make this go away?"

But Sharpton wasn't through yet. "It's a shame that the action is outside the park. New Yorkers are so unforgiving."

Steinbrenner was starting to get mad. "These are bullshit tactics Sharpton, stirring up innocent people. Little kids come to the stadium, you know. Someone could get hurt."

"Why George, you know I can't control the masses. I am just God's humble servant. Why Jesus himself..."

"Cut the crap. What's it going to take to fix this?"

"Well Mr. Steinbrenner," Sharpton stretched out the mister for emphasis, "you know my figure."

"That's bullshit, and you know it. Do you want to work this out, or are you too busy running for mayor?"

"Why George, you insult me," Sharpton had a saddened look on his face. "If that's your position, we might as well take some time to cool off." He got up as if to leave. "I am going to be tied up for the next week or so. Maybe, we should adjourn and talk again at a later date, perhaps in a month or so."

"Get your ass back down in the chair. Again," George took a deep breath, "what is it going to take?"

"Well George, since you insult me with such vile language, you may as well know that the boys are homesick. They are considering sitting out the rest of the season. I have advised them that next year they could try to sign someplace that appreciates humanity, someplace," he paused, "like Boston."

Steinbrenner started to get out of his chair. It looked like he wanted to choke Sharpton. Cashman quickly intervened, "George, why don't you step outside and give me a minute with the Reverend."

After George left, Cashman took a deep breath. He didn't like what he was about to do, but he was used to doing the dirty work. "What would happen, Reverend, if we upped our number to let's say three million each for the rest of the year. The season is half over. That would be a rate of six million for the year." He paused to let it sink in. "And," he hated this part, "we will do what we can to recognize the many things that you have done for the working people of this city."

"You mean graft me," the Reverend feigned outrage.

"Why Al, I mean nothing of the sort. It's just that I appreciate your interest in the boys, the team and the city. We need to get the boys back in the lineup."

"Maybe you should express that appreciation in the press instead of constantly dissing me."

"That's a fair point. Now can we find some common ground?"

"I would be agreeing to highway robbery, but I might be able to get the boys to sacrifice their pride if you made the number three point five."

Cashman flinched. He tried to hide his relief. He knew he was closing in. "George might not go that high, but if I could get him to three and a quarter million, do we have a deal?"

Sharpton assumed the look of a wounded lamb. "It stinks, Cashman, but if that's the best you can do, and if you thank me in the media for saving the Yankees season, I might be able to sell it."

Cashman stuck out his hand. "Good, then we have a deal."

Sharpton smiled and shook hands. Cashman was mildly disgusted, but it had not been as bad as he feared. He was actually proud of his skill in the negotiation. The Boss would be happy. "Maybe, Sharpton wasn't as tough as his reputation," he thought to himself.

As he got up to leave, Sharpton stopped him with a hand to his chest. "Hold on a minute young man. We have agreed on the price, but we still have to work out the terms and other issues."

"What other issues? What the fuck are you talking about?"

"Really, such language for a Christian man."

"What other issues?"

"For one, I have some personal requests. Also, we have a social agenda to discuss."

Cashman kept his composure. "Lay it on me."

"The New York Yankees shame the city with their treatment of colored people. When I look at the front office of the flagship franchise in this city of immigrants, there is not one colored man. We need to correct that problem."

"What are you talking about? Willie Randolph was bench coach last year."

"I am talking about the front office."

"There are only two people in the front office, George and me."

"I am not flexible on this issue. We must put principles ahead of dollars and cents."

The GM was disgusted, but he did a quick mental calculation. A front office worker could be had for $30,000 for the rest of the season. That was peanuts. "It's bullshit, but I will go along with your request. Anything else?"

"Thank you, Mr. Cashman. I am glad you understand that I need to use all my resources to promote God's mission." He looked around to make sure that the door was closed, and no one was listening. "I have two more requests. First, I do need a platform to spread the word of the Lord. Visibility is a powerful thing. I would like to be seen on TV in the owners box with Mr. Steinbrenner, and I would like you to speak to Donald Trump on my behalf. I would like to be one of the guest taskmasters on The Apprentice."

Cashman wanted to say that the team was not interested in promoting his image to conservative Republican voters, but instead he asked, "Do your clients know that you are using them to negotiate on your own behalf?"

“My dealings with my clients are protected by attorney client privilege.”

“I didn’t know that you were an attorney.”

“Small matter, the dealings are still private.”

Cashman knew that George wouldn’t like it, but terms such as these were easier to trade than real money. “If the boy’s money was reduced to say three point one million, I am sure that we could arrange those honorariums for you.”

“That would be satisfactory to all of us. Agreed. Now the last issue,” Sharpton could see that Cashman was getting tense. “Relax Brian. This one will be easy. The boys are a little homesick. They need you to get them a professional to talk to.”

“That shouldn’t be a problem. I will make some calls this afternoon. We will find someone for them.”

“Unfortunately, they don’t want just anyone.”

“Oh, whom do they want?”

“The boys are stressed. They want to talk to Dr. Phil.”

CHAPTER 14

The next morning, the front page of the Daily News had a picture of Al Sharpton and George Steinbrenner shaking hands. The caption read, "The Reverend saves the Yankees' Season." Cashman had to pull some strings to get it done, but the press was always willing to do things for certain considerations. The GM had two valuable currencies to deal with, exclusive interviews and front row play-off tickets.

That night for the Cardinals game, Sharpton and Steinbrenner shared the owners box. Throughout the entire game, they did not speak a word to each other, except when the red light flashed signaling that they were live on camera. Then, the two would smile and feign exchanging pleasantries.

The protests disappeared from the stadium grounds. Hillary Clinton made a statement praising the power of constructive protest. The teamsters union handed out toy trucks to kids under twelve. Crowds filled the seats again. When the Bodine boys came out of the clubhouse tunnel, the fans gave them a rousing cheer.

Donald Trump was quick to get into the act. His writers re-scripted the next episode of the Apprentice. The candidates would compete under Al Sharpton's scrutiny. The task would be to work with an army of inner city kids to refurbish two abandoned churches. One group would rebuild a synagogue, and the other would rebuild a Baptist temple. Al Sharpton felt the theme would help him with New York's Jewish voters. It turned out that there were no abandoned 'inner city' synagogues. A synagogue on the lower east side was substituted. Al Sharpton would be the sole judge of the winning team. His decision would be based on the amount of money raised, the improvements to the facilities and, most importantly, the values imparted on the volunteer kids that participated in the projects.

Donald Trump filmed his testimonial for the episode in front of a Harlem church. After his SWAT team evacuated the area, The Donald faced the camera with one arm around a Latino boy and the other around a black girl. He told the kids that they should dream of some day building the world's biggest skyscrapers with the Trump organization. He announced that the Trump Organization was funding a permanent scholarship to make a different boy or girl honorary bat boy for each Yankee home game. At the end of each year, the bat boy with the best attitude would get a four year scholarship at New York City College. In effect, the Donald was creating a perpetual spin off of the Apprentice.

The sell-out crowd that came to the game that night got their money's worth. Jethro, pitching with an extra day's rest, was unhittable. He struck out the side in each of the first four innings. In the first, he threw only ten pitches. Through seven innings, no Cardinal got on base, and not one even hit the ball out of the infield. Abner was three for five with a home run, and Hoss hit grand slams in the first and third innings. Returning to the dugout after the second homer, Hoss pulled a muscle trying to do a cartwheel for the fans and had to come out of the game. The Yankees were re-energized. Before the game got out of hand, Jorge Posada and Jason Giambi executed a double steal. Gary Sheffield even went from first to third on a ground ball base hit to left.

In the eighth, after Jethro gave up a bloop single, Joe Torre pulled him from the game to rest him for his next start against Chicago. He got a thunderous ovation.

John Sterling said Red Barber would have called it, "An old fashion whupping."

Susan Waldman pondered if the team would lose another game for the rest of the season.

The Yanks scored so many runs that the broadcasters ran out of commercial spots and promotions. By the end of the game, they were speculating on Hoss' dugout exercises and whether or not Jethro even needed a changeup to go with his fastball.

Susan lined up the boys for her post game interview. She wanted to talk about the game, but all they would say was how excited they were to meet Dr. Phil earlier that day. Apparently, Dr. Phil McGraw was a big celebrity in Pea Patch. The interview was short. The boys wanted to get back home quickly so that they could get plenty of rest, not for tomorrow night's game, but because they were going to meet again with the television doctor in the morning.

Chapter 15

From that day on, everything clicked for the New York Yankees. Under daily therapy from their hero, Dr. Phil, the boys relaxed and played even better. Dr. Phil cancelled the rest of his schedule to travel with the team. Apparently, like many men, he was a closet big league wannabe. He had tried out for the Texas Rangers as a kid and had caught a few games in rookie league before he washed out. As he told it, he could field, throw and hit the fastball with power. He claimed he would have been an impact player, but he couldn't hit the curve ball.

As the season approached its final days, the Yankees were so far ahead of the Red Sox that the games were meaningless exhibitions. The stars rested when it didn't affect any of the division races. Joe Torre started to set up his rotation for the playoffs. Traveling with the Yankees was always a media circus, but now, with the games mostly ten-run laughers, reporters wanted to talk to the Bodines and Dr. Phil instead of Jeter and A-Rod. Dr. Phil always gave the press good copy with plenty of one-liners.

In Baltimore, before a day game, he talked about the tough times the boys had growing up without a male figure and how his influence would steady their personal lives. The next day with Jaret Wright pitching, Hoss and Abner both went four for four with two homers apiece. Jethro pinch-hit another homer in the ninth on the way to a fourteen to one victory.

With Abner and Hoss batting behind him, A-Rod was swinging the bat like a MVP. His batting average was up to a career high .367. In the fifth inning against the Orioles, with two runners on base, Alex struck out swinging. Back in the dugout, he threw his helmet against the wall and smashed the water cooler with his bat.

"That's something you don't see often," John Sterling said. "A-Rod is normally such a controlled athlete."

"I think he wants to do his part," Susan Waldman added. "He hates to depend too much on Hoss and Abner."

"That's curious," Sterling broke in. "It looks like Dr. Phil is talking to Alex in the dugout. He's showing him something. I wonder if he's trying to console him."

Susan watched the two of them for about a minute while John went back to the play by play. Then, she broke in. "It looks to me," she said, "that Dr. Phil is giving him some advice. It looks like," she paused for a moment to get up the nerve, "he is telling A-Rod to keep his weight back on his right foot and keep his right elbow up."

"That's what they used to teach in Little League."

Sure enough, the TV cameras were showing Dr. Phil demonstrating to A-Rod the nuances of the big league swing.

"I wonder if that will make A-Rod a big league hitter?" Sterling pondered.

"I wonder how Joe Torre feels about that?" Waldman replied.

It didn't seem to matter though, because in his next at bat, A-Rod hit his longest home run of the season. "We'll have to dig into the story," Sterling said. "I heard a rumor that Dr. Phil was counseling several of the players."

"I heard that rumor, too. Only I heard that he was also working with

George Steinbrenner. Apparently, George had some issues with his mother when he was growing up."

"Well enough of that," Sterling quickly changed the subject, "and back to the action on the field."

After the game, Geraldo Rivera had arranged an exclusive live interview with Abner and Jethro. For some reason, he had not included Hoss. The interview was scheduled to appear on Nightline. The networks promoted it as a chance to find out the real facts behind the biggest baseball story in years. After the show's intro, the cameras panned down to home plate, but instead of Geraldo and the two Bodine boys, only Jethro was standing with the host. Geraldo Rivera was hunched over with his hand on his rib cage. He looked like he was in pain.

"Well, what have you learned about the boys so far?" Stone Phillips led off with the scripted introduction.

"I've learned," Geraldo spoke with a grimace. He was obviously in pain, "that Abner broke up with his girlfriend and…he doesn't like to talk about it." He gasped for air. "So there is hope out there for all you single girls. Now we need to go to commercial."

ABC had shot some special spots just for this occasion. The first one had the Bodines on the beach surrounded by bikini-clad women. As the narrator said, "Let Met Life help you plan for the retirement that you have dreamed about," three of the women fed the boys grapes, and the boys raised a glass to the camera. Abner and Jethro spoke in unison, "We owe it all to Met Life." Hoss was supposed to speak the same line, but he was too busy staring at the models.

Geraldo Rivera had been able to compose himself during the commercial break. He scrapped all the material that he had compiled about Abner and went right to the most sensational issue. "Jethro, let's talk about your brother, Eugene. Can you tell our audience why they call him 'Hoss'?"

Jethro was visibly startled. "I don't really remember. It was a long time ago that we started calling him Hoss. Besides, I think the audience would probably rather talk baseball."

"America wants to know, Jethro. My staff has just spent a week in Pea Patch talking to some of your friends, and they had some pretty interesting stories on the subject. Can you tell me if they are true?"

Jethro paused for a moment. He didn't know what to say. Finally, after a minute, "Well Geraldo, several years ago..."

Before he could say another word, Joe Torre rushed out of the dugout and broke up the interview. "Sorry Geraldo, we have a mandatory meeting in the clubhouse, and then we have to catch a plane to Tampa."

"America wants to know, and they will know, Mr. Torre," Rivera screamed, incensed that his exclusive on national TV was being ruined for a second time. "You can run, but you can't hide. Americans want the truth, and I will see to it that they get it."

"I am sure that you will, Geraldo," Torre said smiling as he spirited Jethro back to the clubhouse. It seemed that everyone in baseball was getting a laugh out of the season. One of the people that was not was Lou Pinella, the manager of the Tampa Devil Rays. Lou, who never got over hard feelings when the Yankees passed over him as manager, had said some nasty things about the Bodine boys and the circus atmosphere of the Yankee season. He had been quoted to say that the Devil Rays would have some surprises of their own the next time the Bombers came to town, which incidentally was tomorrow afternoon.

Chapter 16

Tropicana Field, Tampa Bay:

The first pitch from Tampa Bay's ace, Scott Kazmir, came in high and tight. Jeter sprawled to the dirt to avoid being hit. Immediately, the home plate umpire warned the pitcher and both managers that the next 'purpose' pitch would lead to fines and ejections. Jeter got up and dusted himself off. He had an angry look on his face. His teammates were up on the top steps of the dugout yelling across the field. Even Hoss was getting in the act. Usually calm and reserved, he was making gestures at the Tampa Bay players that no one had ever seen before.

"I don't know what that means," Tim McCarver commented, "but it can't be good."

The commentators for the game were the Fox crew of McCarver and Joe Buck. With all the talk in the press, Fox had changed their schedule to make the Yankees-Devil Rays their game of the week.

The one person on the Yankee bench most offended by the knock down pitch and screaming the loudest was Dr. Phil. The doctor, as a 'special assistant', had taken to wearing a Yankee uniform in the dugout with the number 100 on it. It stood for the one hundred percent effort that in his own mind, he was helping the players achieve. He was standing on the top step, leaning over the rail spewing insults and obscenities with a mix of chewing tobacco. As the umpire was coming over to the dugout, Joe Torre grabbed Dr. Phil by the sleeve and sat him down.

"This might be the first game in history where the team therapist gets ejected," Joe Buck grinned.

"One of many first times in history for this team," McCarver replied.

The next pitch to Jeter was also high and tight. Dr. Phil didn't like it at all. Screaming at the top of his lungs, he took a step onto the field before three Yankees tackled him and dragged him back. The home plate umpire tossed him immediately.

"Well, there you go. The therapist is ejected," McCarver chuckled.

"The papers will have a field day with that one," Buck commented.

In the dugout, the players were agitated, especially the Bodine boys. They had taken a liking to Dr. Phil and were steaming mad that he was thrown out of the game. Fox had set up extra cameras with instructions to follow the boys at all times. They went off camera briefly as they followed their doctor friend into the tunnel. When they came back, they had 'mean dog' looks in their eyes.

"We'll find out what kind of poise the boys have," McCarver said.

"I don't think I would want them mad at me, especially with Jethro on the mound today," Buck replied.

The capacity crowd was enjoying the theatrics. The night before, Lou Pinella had given the papers a sneak peak of things to come. The press played up the theme of Lou's secret strategy to neutralize the Bodines. Lou had invited a couple of good old boys from Pea Patch to the ballpark, and they were given special seats in the first row next to the Yankee dugout. It was theatre at its best. Bill Veeck would have been proud.

The game was surprisingly close, especially since Tampa Bay was the last place team in the division. The Yanks were so incensed by the pregame chatter and brush back pitches, that they were trying too hard. Their batters were over-swinging and Jethro, who usually had perfect control, was missing the plate. Frustration was building.

"I bet that Terry Francona is watching this very closely," Joe Buck said.

"You can be sure that a lot of American League managers are watching this game," McCarver replied.

In the seventh inning, the score was two to two. Jethro had not given up a hit, but he had walked eight. He was still throwing the ball over one hundred and ten miles an hour.

"It is tough enough to face Jethro's heater when he has his control. You're putting your life on the line when his pitches are off the plate," McCarver commented.

Abner and Hoss were clearly off their game. At the plate, they were impatient. Instead of waiting for good pitches to hit, they were chasing balls out of the strike zone, hitting pop ups and weak ground balls. When they made out, the fans from Pea Patch razzed them on their way back to the bench. When they really needed Dr. Phil, he was back in the clubhouse nursing his own ego. Tampa Bay's runs came on two errors by Abner in centerfield in the same inning, his first two errors of the season. He miss-judged a fly ball he should have caught. Then with two outs, he overthrew home plate allowing two runs to score.

When the inning was over, Lou Pinella made a gesture in the dugout as the Yanks were coming off the field. He was signaling to the Pea Patch contingent in the stands. The TV cameras zeroed in on two of them holding up signs. Brian Cashman, who was watching the game at home in New York, immediately recognized one of them as Skeeter, the man who had scammed him with directions on his first trip to Pea Patch. The signs didn't make much sense. They didn't have the normal insults calling the players bums or telling them to go back to the cornfields. Instead, one said in small letters, "Pea Patch Festival 2005." The other said, "Abner, remember the Pea Patch Princess." The boys were angered by the signs and started towards the stands until Joe Torre and a couple of teammates headed them off.

"Whatever Lou Pinella is trying to do, it's working," Joe Buck said. "Everything about their game is off today, their pitching, their hitting and their fielding. Even Hoss' exercises are not the same. He was referring to the pre-batting ritual that so fascinated the public. Since he always had his back to the field, no one could ever see exactly what he was doing. Fox Sports had a special camera trained on him trying to get the story, but the dugout in Tampa Bay had an alcove where Hoss exercised off camera.

"All we can tell is that he is obviously not himself," McCarver said. "His motions are herky jerky, not smooth and fluid as usual."

George Steinbrenner, watching the game from his luxury suite, was not amused in the least. He called the commissioner's office to complain that Tampa was making a travesty of the game. He wanted security to eject the Pea Patch fans from the ballpark, and he wanted Cashman to find out who they were and the significance of what they were doing.

Hideki Matsui led off the top of the ninth. Matsui was always calm under pressure. The advantage of not speaking good English was that he really didn't know all that was going on. He hit a curve ball from Devil Rays' closer Danny Baez into the bullpen to give the Yanks a three to two lead. In the bottom of the ninth, Jethro didn't want to leave the game, but Torre gave the ball to Mariano Rivera. Mariano who normally took a nap on days that Jethro was pitching came in and was mildly effective. He got into a little jam, loading the bases with two outs, but managed to strike out Carl Crawford to save the game.

"This crowd got their money's worth," McCarver said on the post game show. "It might not have been pretty, but it had a little bit of everything. In the end, it was the composure of Joe Torre and Hideki Matsui that prevailed. Jethro Bodine threw eight innings of two run ball and almost lost. We'll have to see if we can find out what in the world the Pea Patch Festival and the Pea Patch Princess are all about."

"You know that every team in the American League will be trying to do the same thing," Buck added.

Chapter 17

George Steinbrenner was having brunch with Donald Trump and Rudy Giuliani at the River Club in New York when his cell phone rang. It was Brian Cashman. George was annoyed. He didn't mind calling Cashman at any hour of the day or night, but he didn't like to be disturbed when he was socializing. "What's so important?" He snapped.

"We have a problem, George."

"Well, handle it. That's what I pay you for."

"You would be upset if I didn't share this one with you."

George stood up and excused himself from the table. He walked out to the empty bar to continue the conversation. "This better be good."

"The Pea Patch Festival is the big social event in Pea Patch. It has been going on for over one hundred years."

"Thanks for the history lesson. Now go on."

"Part of the celebration is that the town votes to pick a young girl to be the Pea Patch Princess for the next year."

"I don't really care. How does this affect me?"

"Last year, Abner's girlfriend, Lila, just missed winning the Princess Pageant."

"Brian, I don't really care about this."

"The three boys got drunk and made real fools of themselves."

"So what."

"Wait, there is more. After the festival, Jethro promised Abner that this year, he would see to it that Lila won."

"Very charming. Why don't you tell this story to the Ladies Home Journal? I am sure their readers would be interested."

"All three of the boys have to be in attendance."

"So give them a couple of days off." George was beginning to get aggravated.

"The dates of this year's festival are October 17th, 18th and 19th. Those are the dates that we play the Red Sox in the LCS."

"Meet me in our midtown offices. I will be there in thirty minutes." George stuffed his cell phone into its holster.

When the Boss told Trump and Giuliani why he had to leave, they both asked if they could help with the problem. They left the restaurant and piled into Steinbrenner's limousine. During the drive, George filled them in on what he knew. Cashman was waiting when they arrived. He looked like he had been up all night. Steinbrenner was still perturbed that his brunch had been cut short by something his employee should have handled. Trump and Giuliani were excited to have a problem to solve. They walked into the office ready to show off their skills.

"We have two issues," Cashman said. "The first is damage control. The Bodines made quite a scene at the festival last year. They were drunk and disorderly. Without going into any of the details, they were also lewd. The publicity would be bad for our team. We can't hush it up. After Saturday's Game of the Week, every tabloid is after the story, and its right out there."

"We'll have to spin it," Rudy cut in. "We'll do a Clinton, like when

Bill and Hillary came clean about their marriage. Barbara Walters owes me one. She can do a special. The boys can cry and tell the people and the fans how sorry they are. I don't think that will be a problem."

"Kind of a 'boys will be boys' thing," Trump added. He was annoyed that he hadn't thought of the solution first. "New Yorkers have great compassion. Especially," he added, "when the boys are playing lights out, and the team is winning."

"I like it," Cashman said. "It might even make the boys seem more human. The fans might relate to that."

"Excellent," Steinbrenner said, enjoying the moment. "What's the second problem?"

"The second problem," Cashman started to explain, almost afraid to say, "is that the boys say they have to attend the Festival."

"They can't. They are under contract. They signed for a lot of money. That's clean and simple."

"It isn't that simple. This is a big deal for them. It's like Yom Kippur for Sandy Koufax."

"We're talking about the LCS with the Red Sox. That's more important."

"I've done some research, George. The Pea Patch Festival is a big deal for them. This isn't going to go away."

"Well, call their agent. Get Sharpton on the phone. He should be able to make them understand breach of contract."

"Sharpton's office already knows about this. They have issued a statement that Sharpton is going to stand behind them. He is calling it an issue of religious freedom."

"It might help get him some votes from the religious right," The Donald broke in. He was growing impatient that Cashman and

Steinbrenner were doing all the talking.

"Well, hell, get the asshole, I mean the Reverend on the phone. We should be able to put a quick end to this."

"We can't, George. The Reverend is in France."

"What's he doing?" Giuliani asked.

"Apparently, he is buying some property on the Mediterranean Coast."

"Let's give the boy's mother a call," George suggested.

"I already tried that," Cashman replied, "but we can't. She is in France with Reverend Sharpton."

The thought of Ma Bodine on vacation with Al Sharpton was mildly repulsive, but Steinbrenner kept his focus. "What about Dr. Phil? Can't he talk some sense into them?"

"I talked to him also. He has been counseling the boys about this very sensitive issue. He told them that they must go back and confront the problems of their past head on."

"But he works for us. The boys aren't paying him. We are."

"That's all he would say. He claims anything else he knows is doctor-patient privilege."

"Remind me to cancel his Christmas bonus."

"Have you talked to the boys?"

"I have. In fact, I have been talking to them all morning. They say they can't even imagine missing the festival."

There was silence. After a couple of minutes, Rudy Giuliani spoke. "I might have a solution," he said. "How many people live in the town of Pea Patch?"

"I think about three hundred."

"What would happen if we bring the Pea Patch Festival and the Pea

Patch Princess and the whole fucking town to New York?"

Donald Trump was upset again. Why didn't he think of that? "That's a great idea, Rudy," he said. "We could get the New York Convention Bureau to pitch in. Another feather in the cap of the greatest city in the world."

"It wouldn't cost that much to fly them all up here," Cashman added.

"Hell no!" The Donald exclaimed. "We will bus them up. It will make for better theatre, besides," he was on a roll now, "it will be considerably cheaper. The Trump Organization would be happy to make all the arrangements. You know that would make it first class. I even know who would be the perfect person to manage the event."

"Who's that Donald?" Steinbrenner asked.

"Omarosa Manigault Stallworth. She was a contestant on the first Apprentice. The press loves her."

"That might work," Giuliani said. He always suspected that The Donald and Omarosa had a 'special' relationship. This confirmed his suspicion.

CHAPTER 18

The next few weeks had not been kind to the Bodines. The Yankees wrapped up the pennant easily, but the games were just a sideshow. The boys appeared on a Barbara Walters exclusive, so that they would not appear on Sixty Minutes or any of the other less controllable news magazines. They talked about their shameful conduct. Jethro talked about the evils of drinking to excess. He admitted to throwing up on the Pea Patch courthouse steps. Abner told all the 'young Yankees in the audience' that he had let them down by screaming profanity after Lila was not named the Princess. Hoss stopped grinning long enough to speak the only full sentence that anyone had heard him utter in three months. Barbara looked him right in the eye as they talked about Hoss urinating on the statue of Hiram Delafield, the founder of the town and the organizer of the first festival. By the time Walters was done with Hoss, only a cold-hearted viewer could not feel sorry for the immature and confused young man. Barbara detailed his upbringing in a poor one-parent home, where he grew up illiterate. She told how he had been self-conscious from the ridicule of the young ladies of Pea Patch over his weight and shy demeanor.

In the pre-interview negotiations, when most of the dialogue was rehearsed and scripted, Walters had tried to explore the issues surrounding the nickname 'Hoss', but that was off limits: Brian

Cashman told Barbara that any questions along those lines would be a deal breaker.

"The public wants to know, and this would be a great time to come clean. The boys could get everything off their chest," Barbara pleaded, but Cashman was firm. In the end, he had to grant Barbara another interview. At the end of the season, when they were ready to talk about the nickname, she would have the exclusive.

When it was finally aired, the show was a masterpiece, perfectly scripted, and perfectly executed. Following the last commercial break, Walters told the boys to close their eyes. After a few seconds of suspense, out walked the boys' two long lost fathers. The Yankees had found Daisy's former husbands in a skid row bar in Atlanta. They had cleaned them up and told them all about their sons. The fathers had decided that it was time to reconnect with their children. They had spent some time with Al Sharpton who had brought Jesus back into their lives. Dr. Phil McGraw had agreed to personally help them confront their past and become the fathers that they now understood they needed to be. The five wept and hugged. It was an emotional epiphany.

The show was a huge success. It garnered the highest Neilsen rating since the last Super Bowl. Emails flooded in from people praying for the whole Bodine clan. America, especially the baseball fans in New York, had decided to forgive and forget. In fact, as Rudy Giuliani had predicted, the show elevated the boys' iconic status to a whole new level.

The Yankees' PR machine sprung to action. Airing immediately after the interview, the team produced a half hour short, called "The Bodine boys, a Treasure of America's Heartland." In addition to highlights, of which there were many, it had the obligatory shots of the boys visiting hospitals, teaching Boy Scouts how to bat and helping to build ball fields in Harlem parks. The highlights themselves were spectacular, Jethro striking out twenty Mariners, Hoss hitting five home runs against Pedro Martinez and Abner scaling the center field wall to take a grand slam away from Barry Bonds.

As the season wound down, the boys had broken several long-standing Yankee records. Jethro had the most consecutive wins, eighteen. Abner had the highest full season batting average, .420 and Hoss had the highest slugging percentage, .715, especially remarkable in that he had only one double and no triples. Jethro had the highest batting average for a designated hitter, and Abner had forty stolen bases against only one caught stealing. In the field, Abner led the league in outfield assists, significant in that after the first month, everybody stopped running against him.

The real story became the Pea Patch Festival. A delegation lead by Omarosa, Rudy Giuliani and The Donald himself, accompanied by a film crew had flown to Pea Patch for meetings with local dignitaries at Town Hall. The mayor convened his council of brothers and half-brothers, and after a short deliberation, they agreed that holding the Festival in New York would be a great way to show off their town to the rest of the world. After the deal was made, Omarosa stayed to negotiate terms and handle the logistics. Donald and Rudy flew back on Trump's jet to Kennedy Airport where Trump had arranged for a special impromptu news conference as they deplaned.

"No problem in business is so large that it cannot be solved where there is a will to succeed," The Donald said in his prepared, 'unprepared speech'. "The Pea Patch Festival, a century of tradition, held in the greatest city in the world, will showcase the undying spirit of small town America, the Pride of the Yankees, and the simple values from the heartland of this country."

Chapter 19

The end of the season was coming fast. Preparations for the Pea Patch Festival were intensifying. Omarosa had built a replica of the Pea Patch Town Hall in Central Park, and crews were putting finishing touches on the bandstand. The Parks Department had planted one hundred ceremonial Magnolia trees, one for each year the festival had been celebrated. Omarosa had lined up celebrities to perform and other celebrities to attend. For two weeks, The Daily News had been running stories about the history of the Festival.

Hiram Delafield had organized the first festival in 1905. It had started as a county fair with baking contests, carnival rides and entertainment. In the thirties, during Prohibition, it became a defiant celebration of the town's independence. The first event was the moonshine tasting contest during which town fathers sampled all the locally produced brands. There were three days of stock car races. The winners were the drivers that could build the biggest gap between themselves and the 'patrol car'. The main attraction was the crowning of the Pea Patch Princess. As legend had it, during the moonshining days, the Princess had the important role of distracting law enforcement while the moonshiners went about their business. In modern times, the Princess Pageant had evolved to reward the 'hottest babe' in the county. There were no talent contests or interviews as in conventional beauty pageants. The Pea Patch Princess was about one thing and one thing only, sex appeal.

As the excitement and hype of this year's festival grew, all of New York City got in the act. Initially, the Pea Patch town council wanted to keep the festival small and private, by invitation only. Subsequently, they had agreed to let Omarosa invite some celebrities to juice up the party and help with funding. In exchange, Omarosa had agreed to split any profits between the Town of Pea Patch and the Trump Organization, which retained exclusive rights to organize and televise the Festival for the next ten years. As the date approached, the Festival became the hottest ticket in town. Omarosa convinced NASCAR to let Jeff Gordon be honorary marshal of the stock car races. Nick Lachey and Willie Nelson were booked to perform concerts. Britney Spears and Christina Aguilera would be special contestants in the Pea Patch Princess contest even though they would not be eligible for the grand prize.

Meanwhile, the New York Yankees were rolling through their opposition building up to the League Championship Series showdown with Boston. The Yanks dispatched California three games to zero in the division series, while the Red Sox beat Chicago with similar ease. Against California, Jethro threw his first no hitter of the season. Hoss set a playoff record by homering in each game of the series and Abner reached base safely in seventeen of his twenty at bats. Mike Scioscia, who had been in baseball for over forty years, said it was the most dominating performance that he had ever seen. In the eighth inning of game three, the broadcasters observed him taping a white towel to a baseball bat. In the ninth inning, he started waiving it towards the Yankees dugout.

"What in the world is he doing? It looks like some kind of signal," John Sterling queried.

"I think he's surrendering," Susan Waldman replied.

The Bombers' wins against California were so one-sided that for the first time in history, Las Vegas refused to take bets for the Yankee-Red Sox series. Jethro pitched game one against Boston, and no one was disappointed. The crowd cheered as he struck out one Red Sox after another. Bob Costas, who was covering the series for NBC, asked Joe Morgan how Jethro compared to the great Bob Gibson, the most feared pitcher of his time. "No contest," was Morgan's reply. "Gibson was great, but this kid is in another league. His fastball has got more pop. His off speed stuff can find every corner of the plate. Gibson was tough and mean, but Jethro Bodine is wicked. When he is on, he is unhittable. The Yankees know that if they can get a run early, the game is pretty much over."

"Gibson wasn't afraid to come inside and keep the hitters off the plate," Costas commented.

"Jethro Bodine doesn't have to come inside to keep hitters off the plate. I hate to say it, but the Red Sox are looking past Jethro. They must feel that they have to win four of the five games that he isn't pitching."

In the fourth inning of game one, Derek Jeter led off with a single, and Alex Rodriguez followed with a walk. After Gary Sheffield lined out, Abner, Hoss and Jethro followed with back to back to back home runs, each one farther than the one before. With the Yanks up by five runs and Jethro pitching in complete control, Terry Francona took most of his regulars out of the lineup. The Bombers went on to win nine to one. With the game out of reach and the play by play meaningless, Costas and Morgan filled the air with what was becoming the usual fare for Yankee games. They speculated about Hoss' pre-bat exercises. They oohed and ahhed as Abner threw bullets from center to warm his arm between innings. "I only wish Jackie Robinson could have tested that arm," Morgan commented. They poked fun at Hoss. "It's hard to believe that someone so short and squat can hit the ball so far," Costas said.

"Seeing is believing," Morgan replied after Hoss hit his second tape measure homer into the left field stands.

"I don't know if anything could top this," Costas said after the game. Joe Morgan nodded in agreement.

But as they say in the circus, "The best was yet to come."

Chapter 20

Cletus Barnes sat in his office. It was a big day for the Yankees. First, it was game seven of the League Championship Series. Just as Joe Morgan had predicted, the Yankees had won game four with Jethro pitching and game six with Randy Johnson. The Sox had squeezed out victories in games two, three and five. It was also the final day of the Pea Patch Festival. Today, they would name the Pea Patch Princess.

For Cletus, it had been an interesting couple of weeks. To fulfill his promise to Al Sharpton, Brian Cashman had promoted Cletus to 'Special Assistant to the General Manager'. He had been given his own office, complete with phone, desk and access to the team secretaries. Behind his desk was a framed picture of Cletus between Sharpton and Jesse Jackson from the cover of Black Entertainment Magazine. They were all wearing Yankee caps. The caption said, "At the table at last." The article praised the hard work of the civil rights leaders in promoting diversity and opportunity for minorities.

Cletus didn't like his new job. He preferred the old job of helping out around the clubhouse, but the money was good and being a 'role model for young blacks' as the magazine called him, had its benefits.

His current assignment was liaison with Omarosa for the final day of the Festival. He was in charge of providing transportation for the boys from Central Park to Yankee Stadium. The plan was to have a limo pick them up immediately after the crowning of the Princess. Since the Princess vote had been scheduled for ten o'clock in the morning, and the game didn't start until eight at night, there was plenty of time. Cletus picked up his phone and dialed Omarosa's cell. He got her voice mail and left a message for Omarosa to call him. It was the third message he had left this morning.

In Central Park, the first two days of the Festival had been a smashing success. The festivities opened with a Willie Nelson concert that over one hundred thousand attended. The park was closed to traffic for the stock car races. Jeff Gordon graciously backed off his lead feigning engine trouble to allow a local boy to win the event. Press passes were issued to writers from around the world. Newspapers wrote more about the Pea Patch Festival than about Prince Charles, who was making his first trip to New York with his new bride. No one promoted big events better than the Trump Organization, and no city could create flair and excitement like New York. Pea Patch's share of the combined profit from concessions, souvenir sales and advertising was over five million dollars in the first two days alone. Donald Trump was even talking about holding next year's festival in Atlantic City. The two remaining feature events were the moonshine judging contest and the Princess Pageant. Hoss and Jethro were honorary judges of the moonshine contest. The events were right on schedule.

As the moonshine contest was concluding, Al Sharpton, the honorary chief taster, announced the names of the remaining entries, Huckleberry Brew, Hot Mash and Bo's Pride. The judges were given a sample of each brand and a bucket for spitting the samples into after they were tasted. Omarosa was to supervise Hoss and Jethro to make sure they were only tasting and not consuming the moonshine. Brian

Cashman insisted that she attend to it personally as it was too important a task to delegate.

Over at the Princess venue, the finalists were Abner's girlfriend, Lila, another local girl named Dixie, and the honorary finalists, Britney Spears and Christina Aguilera. All of them were wearing their skimpiest outfits that they had saved for the finals. The crowd had overflowed the temporary staging area set up in the park. Closed circuit carried the pageant to convention halls around the city. At the last minute, Omarosa had arranged to have the finals carried live on Spike TV. To make the deal more marketable, Donald Trump and George Clooney had been recruited as special emcees. The crowd hooted and cheered as the finalists came on stage. The audience was expecting quite a show, and the contestants lived up to the expectations. Britney wore a halter-top and leather chaps covering very brief panties. Christina wore a cowgirl outfit with denim jeans and a red checkered shirt. Not to be outdone, Lila's and Dixie's outfits had been specially designed by Tommy Hilfiger. Both of the girls were in great shape and very attractive to begin with. Dixie was wearing loose bib overalls with nothing underneath. She had a red scarf in her hair. Lila was all Daisy Duke, short, tight hot pants and a three button white shirt. The final event of the Pageant was quite simple. After being escorted across the stage by Trump and Clooney, the four danced to fiddler's music while the panel eliminated them one by one. It had been pre-arranged to eliminate Spears and Aguilera at the same time. As planned, they both feigned disappointment and left the stage. After two more minutes of dancing, Trump escorted Lila, and Clooney led Dixie to the judge's stand for the final announcement. The crowd hushed. Flashbulbs popped and crackled. The judges handed their cards to the mayor.

The Mayor spoke, "The Pea Patch Princess will have the great distinction of representing our fair town to the outside world and carrying out all the honorary duties as described by our traditions. The Pea Patch Princess for next year will be the lovely…" the mayor paused enjoying his two minutes of celebrity, "May we have a drum roll please." An assistant whispered in his ear that there was no band to perform a drum role. "In that case, we will announce the winner right after this commercial." He had seen Ryan Seacrest do this many times on American Idol. The assistant whispered to him that there were no commercials scheduled. "In that case without any further ado, the winner of this year's pageant is the lovely…Lila."

The crowd yelled and screamed. No one yelled and screamed louder than Abner. As the camera zoomed in, there were tears in his eyes.

CHAPTER 21

Cletus hung up the phone, picked up his coat and hurried out of his office. He had just finished talking to Brian Cashman. It was four o'clock, and the Bodines were nowhere to be found. Everyone, including Joe Torre, was beginning to panic. It was almost time for pre-game batting practice. Joe didn't like the thought of game seven without his superstars. The prospects of winning were not good with Randy Johnson pitching on one day's rest.

Brian Cashman was livid. "Where the hell are they? Where the hell is Omarosa? What the hell is going on?" He tried Omarosa's cell, but kept being sent to an annoying voice mail. He tried to call Steinbrenner who was also at the festival, but his phone was turned off. He told Cletus to meet him in the parking lot. They would go find the boys themselves. Before he left, he told his secretary to dial Omarosa's cell phone continuously. As they sped towards Central Park in his Mercedes, Brian lectured Cletus, "You had one job and one job only to get the boys back to the ball park. Omarosa had the job to keep her eye on them. This is no way to go into game seven."

In Central Park, the Festival was winding down. After she had been crowned Princess, Abner led Lila through the ceremonial first dance. Donald Trump, George Clooney and George Steinbrenner graciously agreed to dance with Dixie, Britney and Christina. Afterwards, the floor opened up for the rest of the invited guests. For the 'A' list and 'A' list wannabes, this was an event made in Heaven. As they paraded around in skimpy outfits with other 'A' listers on national TV, all in the name of charity, they knew it couldn't get any better.

When Cletus and Cashman arrived, the music was loud and the crowd frenzied. They couldn't find anyone who knew the whereabouts of their ballplayers. The volunteers had succumbed to the excitement of the moment, not to mention the moonshine. On the dance floor, the best in New York was out in full force. Woody Allen was dancing with a grinning Jessica Simpson. Brad Pitt and Angelina Jolie were bouncing up and down. Justin Timberlake was doing the two-step with Lisa Marie Presley. Barbara Walters was hoofing it up with Puff Daddy. Al Sharpton was going wild with a nearly naked Pamela Anderson. Cashman finally found Steinbrenner dancing with Ashley Simpson. The Boss was not happy that his dance had been interrupted. When Cashman told him what was going on, he was furious. Immediately, they set out in search of their players. They found a policeman standing next to one of the Magnolia trees and asked him to put out an APB to find the Bodines. The policeman was apathetic. He was watching the celebrities on the dance floor and didn't notice whom he was talking to.

"Do you know who I am?" Steinbrenner asked indignantly.

"Wait till the end of this number, sir," the officer replied.

Steinbrenner wrote down his badge number and huffed off. Fortunately, they caught sight of Rudy Giuliani and Mayor Bloomberg standing behind the stage. "Rudy, we have a big problem. We need your help right away." They explained the situation.

"I think I can help," Mayor Bloomberg said. He barked some orders into his cell phone. “If those boys are still in New York, my boys will find them.”

Cashman looked at his watch. It was five o’clock, only three hours to game time.

Chapter 22

At five thirty, a beat cop spotted Omarosa's limousine. With a police escort, Brian, George, Cletus and Rudy sped to the scene. The stretch limo with license plates, 'True Apprentice', was parked behind a bush half-hidden from the road. Steinbrenner got out of the Mercedes and ran towards the limo. As he approached, he noticed that the windows were steamy. He rapped on the window. There was no answer. He rapped again and again. Finally, he heard Omarosa's voice.

"Who the hell is it, and this better be important."

"This is George Steinbrenner. Get your ass out of the car now."

There was some stirring around inside. After a minute, Omarosa appeared. She was disheveled, and her clothes were a mess. The top buttons of her blouse were unfastened. Omarosa noticed their stares. She quickly buttoned her blouse.

"Hello, Mr. Steinbrenner. What can I do for you?" she asked as if nothing was out of the ordinary.

"We don't have time for small talk. Where the hell are the boys?"

Omarosa knew she was in trouble and immediately went on the offensive."Mr. Steinbrenner, a simple thank you might be in order. The festival was a huge success. Everything went as planned to the smallest detail."

"Yeah, yeah, yeah, now where the hell are the boys?"

"Mr. Steinbrenner, please. Your language."

"Sorry Omarosa, let me rephrase. Where the fuck are my ball players?"

Omarosa came right back at him, "What's the matter George? Do you feel threatened by a successful black woman? Are you some kind of racist?"

Meanwhile, Brian Cashman felt that he needed to look in Omarosa's limousine. He wasn't sure that he wanted to see who might be inside, but he needed to check just in case it was one of his players. He opened the driver's door and peaked in. Passed out in the back seat was his old friend, Skeeter. When the cool air from outside hit him, Skeeter sprung to attention. The first thing he did was feel for his wallet. Next, he quickly sat up and saw Cashman peering in the door. His face relaxed. He gave Brian a thumbs-up and a big wink. Then, he zipped his fly, closed his eyes and went back to sleep. As upset as Cashman was, he couldn't help a little chuckle.

Steinbrenner was ready to kill Omarosa. He took two steps towards her with his hands up like he was going for her throat. Rudy Giuliani moved in between them.

"George, step back and think clearly. We've only got two hours to game time. We need her alive."

Steinbrenner paused and loosened his tie.

"Allow me," Giuliani said. "Now, Omarosa, what was the plan. Do you have any idea where they are? How were you keeping track of them?"

"They are all carrying GPS units. If Mr. Steinbrenner had just asked me nicely, I would have told him. This Garmin," she handed a receiver to the ex-mayor, "will lead you right to them." Rudy grabbed the device. Off they went again.

Omarosa waited for a second. When she saw that no one was watching her, she climbed back into the limo.

Steinbrenner looked at his watch. It was five minutes of six. "Find my players quickly," he said. "I've got to get back to the stadium."

The Garmin led them right to the boys. They had wandered a couple of miles from the festival uptown towards Harlem. They were sitting around a fire barrel with a couple of winos passing around a jug of the prize-winning moonshine. Jethro was amusing himself with a harmonica. Abner was passed out. Hoss was talking up a storm.

Cashman looked at his watch, and he looked at Rudy. Eighty minutes to game time and three drunken superstars, they didn't cover this in general managers school.

"Well, hello Mr. Cashman," Hoss bellowed.

Abner stirred just enough to say, "Howdy."

"Welcome to my old Kentucky Home," Jethro sung out of key.

Brian took the jug of moonshine and handed it to one of the winos. "Please have this with my compliments," he said.

"Thank you, sir," the wino answered. Then, noticing the Yankee cap, he recognized the GM. "Mr. Cashman, sir, if you need a second baseman, I'm your dog. I can hit, and I can run. I can turn a mean double play." He rambled on, "I used to play in the Roslyn Little League. I caught for Jay Prosnitz."

"Thank you, sir," Cashman handed the drunk his card. Call me before spring training. Otherwise, I will call if we need you."

As the police loaded the boys into the back seat of Brian's Mercedes, Hoss yelled out, "Bring Jackson along."

"We're in a little bit of a hurry, Hoss," the GM replied.

"Bring Jackson along. He's my best buddy."

Cashman had no time to argue. "Load him up, too, boys," he said to one of the cops. With sirens blazing, the procession sped off to Yankee Stadium.

"We found them, and we are on our way," Rudy told George over his cell phone.

"Can you get them here by game time?"

"Yes, but we have a little bit of a problem, George."

"What's that?"

"You better get some coffee brewing. The boys are dead drunk."

"Mr. Steinpeter, this is Eugene. How the hell you doing?" Hoss yelled from the backseat.

"Just get them to the ball park," the Boss ordered before he hung up.

When Joe Torre heard the news, he fought off the urge to panic. "Think clearly," he told himself. He remembered a story of Yankee lore from back in the sixties. Mickey Mantle, the team's best and most popular player, had gone on an all-night binge after a ball game. The next day, he showed up at the park hung over. He was wearing the same clothes from the day before. He had not slept. The Yanks had a scheduled double-header. It was one hundred and five degrees at the start of the first game. When Mantle walked into manager, Ralph Houk's office, the star expected to be benched and lectured, but Houk, an ex-marine, had a better idea. He made Mantle play every inning of the double-header in center field as punishment. The irony was that Mantle went seven for ten that day with two home runs. Torre thought about the story as he played with his lineup card. Did he dare play the three drunken stars in game seven of the League Championship Series. "What the hell," he thought to himself. "I can't win without them. I have nothing to lose."

CHAPTER 23

The convoy arrived at the ballpark fifteen minutes before game time. The Yankees had cleared the press out of the clubhouse. The sole reporter allowed was Sam Borden. He had been promised an exclusive and could be counted on to handle the matter discretely. Fox TV was furious. They had to cancel their pre-game interviews. In the press box, Joe Buck was breaking the news.

"There is a story spreading that some of the Yankees are missing. The word is that it might be the Bodines. They might not have returned from the Pea Patch Festival."

"Sources tell us that they might have been drinking to excess," Tim McCarver added. "That might make things very interesting, especially if Jethro can't pitch."

"We haven't seen him warming up in the bull pen, but we can't seem to get any details at this time. As soon as we do, we will pass them on."

As invasive as the New York media could be, they had a code for protecting their superstars. Tomorrow, the city papers would crucify the whole organization, especially if the Yanks lost the game, but for now the story was a local matter to be shared only with the fraternity of city reporters. Fox would not get the full story.

"Wait a minute, Tim," Joe Buck cut in. "We have an update from the clubhouse. Apparently, everything is OK. The full team is in the park.

The Bodines were visiting a terminally ill boy at Sloane hospital and were held up by some heavy traffic. I guess Jethro is warmed up and ready to go."

"Great!" McCarver replied. "We will return for game seven of the LCS, the National Anthem and the first pitch right after these messages."

In the Yankee clubhouse, the mood was somber. Cletus was pouring coffee and water down the boys' throats. "We've got to get them hydrated quickly," Gene Monahan, the trainer, had instructed.

Joe Torre realized that it was no time for a lecture. "How do you feel, Ab?" he asked. "Can you play?"

"Gee, I'm fine, Zeke," Abner replied to his manager. "I don't have to be sober to pitch against no damn Yanks."

"You're playing for the Yanks," Derek Jeter interjected. He was standing by observing the situation. "and you're not pitching. You are playing centerfield."

"He means northerners," Jethro hummed. "He doesn't really like Yanks, I mean northerners." Jethro had put his shirt on backwards and for a moment was confused. Cletus came to his rescue and helped him get it on straight.

Abner didn't have anything more to say. He was a passive drunk. Meanwhile, Hoss couldn't stop talking. He was running around the clubhouse wearing his jock strap on his head and nothing else. He was trying to talk to Gary Sheffield. "Did I ever tell you about the time my third grade class went to the chicken farm? My, they had rows and rows and rows of chickens all in them cute little cages."

Gary gave him a shut-up-and-leave-me-alone look. During his career, Sheffield took the game and his pregame preparation very seriously. Hoss continued, "Miss Holly, our teacher, had the biggest knockers you have ever seen. We kept dropping our papers so she would bend over and pick them up. I thought for sure her boobs would fall out."

Sheffield had enough. He gave Hoss a shove and sent him tumbling. Abner and Jethro were drunk, but they were fiercely protective. They jumped on Sheffield, and the fight was on.

Jethro took a swing and caught the right fielder in the mouth. Hideki Matsui jumped in and aimed a karate kick at the pitcher's head. Jethro blocked it with his right arm. He let out a blood-curdling yell and grabbed his forearm. He slumped over into a chair screaming. Meanwhile, Hoss was laughing hysterically. While no one was paying attention, he wandered into the bathroom and was fixing to drink some mouthwash when Cletus stopped him. With total chaos in the locker room, there was only five minutes to game time.

Joe Torre was trying to restore order when the clubhouse door boomed open. In walked Phil McGraw and Ma Bodine.

"Gentlemen, gentlemen," Phil said in his southern drawl. "Get a hold of yourselves." He walked over to Abner and gave him a pat on the butt. "Take a deep breath and count to three." Abner immediately smiled and relaxed. He liked it when he got Phil's undivided attention.

"Jethro," he walked over to the big right-hander who was grimacing and holding his arm. "Jethro, Jethro, Jethro, young man, history won't tolerate anything but your best effort." Jethro had no idea what that meant, but he beamed at what he thought was a compliment.

He was walking over to Hoss, but Daisy had got there first. "Take that silly thing off your head you dumb bastard." She whacked him across the back of his neck with her open hand. "Get your uniform on, and get your head out of your ass." She turned to Jethro. "Now grow up and get dressed."

"I can't pitch, momma, my arm hurts too bad," Jethro sobbed.

"Just get your ass out on the field you dumb son of a bitch," she replied. "Abner can pitch today."

"I thought you all said Abner didn't know how to pitch," Torre cut in. The media would kill him if he sent a first time starter to the mound for game seven.

"Oh hell," Daisy replied. "He's the best pitcher you've ever seen. He just doesn't like to pitch. He's too damn lazy. He'll do just fine, especially if he's had too much to drink."

"Gentlemen," Phil McGraw walked into the center of the locker room. Dr. Phil had been waiting for this moment all of his life. He was about to give the New York Yankees a pep talk before game seven against Boston. He paused a minute soaking up the drama. There were a lot of things that he had prepared to say, but instead, he said simply, "You are about to play baseball for New York against Boston. Never again in your lives will you do anything as important!" He paused for a moment to let his profound remark sink in and then started to shake all the players' hands.

Joe Torre had prepared some remarks also, but he could feel that now was not the time or the place. "Guys," Joe said, "we've got to win this game. We've been through too much shit to lose."

Chapter 24

"And the Yankees take the field," Bob Sheppard announced. "We have a change in the starting lineup. Abner Bodine will be pitching and batting fourth. Bernie Williams will be playing center field."

"Torre must be crazy," John Sterling said away from his mike, "or maybe there is some truth to the rumors floating around."

"I see Jethro on the bench, and he has some ice on his arm," Susan Waldman added. "This has got to be good news for the Red Sox."

"We'll see if we can get some kind of report on Abner. I have no idea what kind of stuff he throws."

Over in the Fox booth, Tim McCarver, an ex-catcher, was paying special attention to Abner's warm up throws. "The Jugs Gun has got him at one ten," Tim observed. "It is going to be tough on the hitters if he can keep up that speed."

"He's got his glove over his mouth. What's he doing?" Joe Buck queried.

"It looks like he just threw up," McCarver replied. "I guess he's got pregame jitters like everyone else."

'Who can blame him," Buck said. "It's game seven."

The first pitch to Johnny Damon was a strike right down the middle. The next two flew way over his head.

"It seems like Abner might have some control issues," Buck

commented. "He looks pretty wobbly out there."

The next pitch was a fast strike on the outside corner. Another pitch was low. Damon whiffed at the payoff pitch for the first out.

"Is Abner doing a dance out there?" Buck asked.

"It looks like he is singing a song, too," McCarver replied. "I wonder if he does that after every strikeout?"

"We'll find out pretty soon."

The next batter was Edgar Renteria. Abner walked him on four pitches. None were even close to the plate. He walked Manny Ramirez on four pitches, also, bringing Mel Stottlemyer to the mound. After a quick meeting, Mel returned to the dugout. Whatever he said must have worked because he blew David Ortiz away on three fastballs for the second out.

"What did you tell him?" Joe Torre asked his pitching coach.

"I told him Lila said he couldn't do it," Mel replied.

"Good thinking," Joe said.

"Then he told me," Mel continued, "that he wanted a hit of White Lightning if he struck out the side. We've got a flask in your office. We've got to play this one out the way it's dealt."

On the field, Abner walked Trot Nixon to load the bases before striking out Jason Varitek on the next three pitches.

"Is he playing with them?" Joe Buck asked. "He is pitching like a drunken sailor."

Tim McCarver did not say anything. He had a puzzled look in his eyes.

The Yankees jumped on Curt Schilling in the first inning. Derek Jeter led off with a single, and Alex Rodriguez walked. Gary Sheffield lined a single to left, and the Bombers were up one to nothing with

Abner coming to the plate and Hoss on deck. The Fox TV crew with the team's permission had put a small camera in the corner of the Yankees' dugout to cover Hoss' pre-bat ritual. In all the excitement, the home team had forgotten it was there.

"Hoss Bodine has been quite an enigma," McCarver announced, "incredible bat speed, a great eye at the plate. All you young hitters out there might want to watch him limber up. What do you think he does, Joe? Today, we will find out."

"My thought is that it is some type of relaxation ritual," Joe responded, "maybe meditation, maybe some isometrics. Let's find out. Let's go to the cameras."

All of a sudden, McCarver started laughing. The camera quickly cut to a commercial. "It looks to me," McCarver said under his breath when he knew that he was off the air, "that Hoss is urinating. So much for our special camera."

"Something else," Joe Buck said with a chuckle. He knew he was off the air, too. "We just might know why they call him Hoss."

Back on the field, Abner struck out on a breaking pitch that bounced twenty feet in front of the plate. As he was walking back to the dugout, he started strumming his bat like a guitar. "He doesn't look like himself," Joe Buck observed. Tim McCarver had been around for a long time. He didn't say anything, but he was pretty sure he knew what was going on.

Hoss came up to bat next. "Hoss Bodine led the American League in slugging percentage," Buck announced. "He is a shy person. No one really knows what he is about. He could give the Bombers a big lead if he comes through here."

Hoss walked up to the plate, but instead of his normal shy demeanor, he was chatting with the home plate ump and Jason Varitek, the Red Sox catcher. He stood and watched strike one on the inside corner. Stepping out of the box, he started talking to the ump until he was ordered back to the plate. He stood and watched strike two come right down the middle.

"I would have guessed he would have sent that one to the moon," Buck said.

Strike three was another fastball and still no swing. On his way back to the dugout, Hoss stopped to talk to a blond in a box seat next to the dugout.

"What's going on?" Buck asked.

"It looks like he's asking her to marry him," McCarver replied.

Joe Torre had a big decision. If he could hold on long enough, the boys might sober up. If he took them out of the game, he couldn't put them back in. "Shit," Joe thought to himself, "I would rather be drunk than the way I am now. As Mel said, let's just play the cards the way they were dealt."

The game continued.

CHAPTER 25

After seven innings, the score was still one to nothing. Curt Schilling was pitching a strong game. Hoss and Abner had helped him out of several jams, striking out and leaving runners on base. Abner was throwing a no hitter with fifteen strikeouts, but he had walked twelve and thrown over one hundred and sixty pitches. The boys were far from sober. Hoss was playing with the spare bats in the dugout trying to build a house of cards. Every few minutes they would fall with a loud clatter. After every out, Abner continued to sing off key. Jethro wasn't much better. Whenever the Yanks got a hit, he would pretend he was a cheerleader and go into a stupid routine. The rest of the team was annoyed. Torre made them sit by themselves at the end of the bench.

In the top of the eighth, Abner got the first two outs on soft grounders, but then walked the next three batters to load the bases. "Mariano time," Joe said to Mel. "Get him up in the pen." Mariano Rivera had pitched two full innings in each of the last two games, and his arm was tired. Joe had hoped that he would only need him for one inning at the most, but with two outs in the eighth and the game on the line, he had no choice. Mel Stottlemyre hung up the bullpen phone. "He's getting ready as quick as he can, but his arm is stiff. He'll need an extra minute or two to warm up."

The extra minute proved costly for the bombers. Bill Mueller lined a fastball into the gap, clearing the bases, and the Bosox were ahead three to one. When Joe went out to the mound to change pitchers, Abner was trying to balance his cap on his nose. Joe would have loved to send him packing, but his spot was due up in the bottom of the inning. He sent him to center field and inserted Rivera in Bernie William's spot in the lineup. Mariano got Varitek to hit a slow grounder between Giambi and Robinson Cano. Jason scooped it up and flipped to Mariano covering first for the third out.

Fox was about to go to commercial when there was a loud reaction from the Yankee fans. Mariano Rivera was lying on the ground next to first base holding his ankle. "Oh my!" McCarver said looking at the replay. "He stepped on the side of the base. He might be done for the day."

"More when we come back from commercial," Joe Buck said.

The whole Yankee team was standing around watching Gene Monahan attend to their fallen closer. He tried to get up, but could not put any weight on his right foot. Flash Gordon got up in the bullpen to get ready for the top of the ninth.

As Johnny Damon and Manny Ramirez were jogging to their outfield positions, Abner was taking his time coming in from center, picking clovers from the grass and sticking them into his hatband. Manny and Johnny didn't notice that Abner was within earshot. "This ought to show those hillbillies," Manny said to Damon. "They're nothing but white trash."

"You got that right," Damon replied, "and I never thought I would say this, but I bet their mama wears army boots."

They had no idea that Abner Bodine had heard what they said. Abner was standing frozen still. Whoever coined the phrase, "sobering experience," must have had something like this in mind. The jester look was off Abner's face as he ran in. By the time he got to the dugout, his expression was stone cold. While the rest of the Yanks were watching Mariano get to his feet and be helped off the field, Abner called Jethro and Hoss to the side and told them what he had heard. The color came back to Jethro's cheeks. His smile turned into a scowl. Hoss stopped babbling and took a couple of steps up the dugout stairs with a bat in his hand before his brothers restrained him. Neither the Yankee players nor the play by play announcers noticed anything. They were busy talking about Mariano's ankle. Just before cutting to commercial, Tim McCarver saw that the boys were talking. "Joe, look into the dugout," he said, "Jethro just took the ice off his elbow."

"It's the eighth inning, and we're behind the Red Sox," Jethro said to his brothers.

"I don't give a shit about the inning. Those bastards are going to pay for talking that way about mama," Abner replied.

Hoss wasn't clowning around anymore. He was grinning, but it was a hateful grin of a demon, not the playful grin of the town fool.

Keith Foulke, the Red Sox closer, came in to pitch the bottom of the inning. The Red Sox were six outs away from going to the World Series. Back in the dugout, Joe Torre was looking at his lineup card. Abner, Hoss and Mariano's spot were due up. On the bench, he had Andy Phillips, Bubba Crosby and Luis Soho available to pinch hit. None of them were hitting for much of an average.

While Foulke was finishing his warm-up tosses, George Steinbrenner came into the dugout with Phil McGraw. "Dr. Phil wants to talk to the boys," George said. "He can help them focus."

The boys were standing with their helmets on and bats in their hands. "Tell him to sit down and stay out of the way," Abner said in a cold hard manner.

"Boys, this is a big moment in Yankee history," the Boss replied. "Dr. Phil can help."

"If he wants to help, tell him to go away. We've got some work to do," Jethro said. He had a mad-dog look in his eyes.

"You need to do what I say," Steinbrenner said. "Remember, I am the Boss."

"With all due respect, boss," Hoss said, catching everyone by surprise as it was the first time anyone had heard him talk, "shut the fuck up, and get the hell out of the dugout."

For a second, no one stirred. Then Dr. Phil took George by the arm. "Remember what we discussed about control issues," he said as he led the Boss off.

After a second of silence, some of the Yanks started to smile. Many of them had wanted to say that to George for years, but there wasn't any time to savor the moment. It was game seven.

Joe Torre didn't have a chance to think about pinch-hitting. Abner was already on his way to the plate, and Hoss was in the on deck circle. Besides, in his fifty years in baseball, Joe had seen the look in their eyes before, and he knew what it meant.

Abner dug in for the first pitch. Joe Buck was saying that he was 0 for three for the day with three strikeouts, when Foulke delivered. Wham!

Buck screamed into the microphone, "There's a home run for the ages. It's, it's…out of Yankee stadium, the first time in history that a fair ball has been hit out of Yankee stadium. This stadium is over eighty years old and never, not Babe Ruth, not Lou Gehrig, not Joltin Joe not

Reggie Jackson has anyone ever hit one out of the ballpark. Mickey Mantle came close, but this is history. The Yankees have cut the lead to 3-2."

As Abner rounded second at full speed, he started yelling at Manny Ramirez in left.

"What's he saying?" Joe Buck asked.

"I can't tell," McCarver replied, "but it looks like something about army boots."

Hoss was up next. Foulke's first pitch was a high, hard one, right under his head. Hoss hardly moved, lifting his chin half an inch to let the ball pass. "That's concentration," McCarver said. "Watching him stand in like that, I would say there is nothing to those rumors that are floating around the ball park."

"Hoss is 0 for three today," Buck added. "I don't think he has swung the bat in his previous at bats."

Foulke delivered the next pitch. Whack!

"Oh my God, there it goes it goes again. It's…out of here. Two balls out of Yankee Stadium in a row. This one further than the last. Unbelievable."

For a second, Tim McCarver was speechless. Then, he said, "The late, great Red Barber would have said 'O doctor'."

The game was tied three to three.

Before Joe Torre could make a move, Jethro grabbed his bat and headed to the plate. "Bodine for Rivera, he told the home plate ump."

"He is still rubbing his right arm," Buck announced. "It looks like he is going to bat left handed. I didn't know he was a switch hitter. Can he make it three in row?"

They had a quick answer. On the first pitch, he laid a bunt down the third base line. There wasn't even a throw. Gary Sheffield was up next.

On the first pitch, Jethro broke for second. The Red Sox pitched out, but Jethro beat the throw easily. On the next pitch, they pitched out again, but to no avail. Jethro stole third. On the third pitch, the Red Sox threw a third pitchout in a row. Jethro stayed on third base. He looked into the Red Sox dugout and pointed his index finger to his head.

"It looks like he is calling them out," Joe Buck said.

"What in the world has got into the Bodine boys?" McCarver replied.

The next pitch to Sheffield was low for ball four. As Varitek threw it back to his pitcher, Jethro broke for the plate. He caught Foulke off guard. By the time the pitcher noticed, it was too late. Jethro scored, and the Yanks were up four to three.

"That's a play you only see in Little League," Buck said excitedly. "That's the first time anyone has stole home in the playoffs since you did Tim."

"Two balls hit out of the stadium and a steal of home in the same inning. This is one for the history books," McCarver added.

"Do you think Terry Francona will bring Myers in to face Matsui?" Buck asked.

"I think he will have to," McCarver replied. "Keith Foulke is walking off the field."

Sure enough, Foulke started walking to the dugout before his manager even got to the mound. "I guess he had enough, and who can blame him," McCarver said.

Mike Myers came in and got the next three outs without allowing a base-runner. The game went to the top of the ninth. Flash Gordon was finishing his warm up pitches when the bullpen coach told him to sit down. Jethro Bodine was going to pitch the ninth inning.

"This is a big gamble," John Sterling said on the Yankee radio network. "Flash Gordon is the more experienced reliever."

"Torre needs to let Jethro close the game," Susan Waldman replied. "This is bigger than the game. Let's see how Jethro does with only a nine pitch warm-up. That's tough on a starter."

In the top of the ninth, the Red Sox were sending up the heart of their order, Manny Ramirez, David Ortiz and Jason Varitek. Jethro took the ball and pounded his glove. He barked something to Ramirez who was standing in the batters box.

"What is he saying to him?" Joe Buck asked.

"It looks like he is saying only fastballs," McCarver replied. "This is really mano-a-mano. What's got into him?"

The first pitch was a called strike one. It measured one hundred and twenty on the Jugs Gun. Ramirez made contact on the second pitch, fouling it back as his bat shattered. After grabbing a new bat, Ramirez dug in and clenched his teeth as Jethro let loose. It was a slow change. Ramirez swung before the ball was halfway to the plate for strike three. "So much for only fastballs," Buck said.

David Ortiz came up next. He took a mighty cut and missed for strike one. He swung and missed again, strike two. On the third pitch, Ortiz was looking for the change and got the fastball instead. He started walking back to the dugout before the ump could even call strike three. The Yankees were one out away from the World Series.

CHAPTER 26

The noise level was deafening. The police were preparing to come onto the field anticipating a Yankee victory. As Jason Varitek dug into the box, he started yapping at Jethro on the mound.

"What's he saying?" Joe Buck asked.

"I can't say for sure, but it looks like he is making some reference to Jethro's mother," McCarver answered.

"That might not be the smartest thing to say to someone with a fastball like Jethro's," Buck said.

"Especially someone who is a little unstable," McCarver added.

Varitek's strategy paid off quickly. The first pitch came in hard and inside. The Red Sox captain stepped into it and took it square in the ribs. He went down like a buffalo that was shot with a high caliber rifle.

"That's one way to get on base," McCarver commented as Varitek lay on the ground writhing in pain. "Talk about the ultimate 'taking one for the team'."

Varitek lay on the ground for five minutes before the Red Sox training staff got him up and back to the dugout. The speedy Brian Roberts went to first base representing the tying run. The Red Sox bench starting yelling threats and obscenities at Jethro on the mound. Manny Ramirez was the most vocal. He was standing on the top step screaming. Jethro was screaming back, "Bring it on. I am right here."

With his finger, he was beckoning for Manny to come to the mound.

The umpires walked back and forth to both dugouts trying to keep the peace. The crew chief ordered the police to take the field to control the crowd. "Both of the benches are warned," the home plated ump shouted. "Joe, tell your boy that if anything comes in too close, he is out of the game."

Dr. Phil had returned to the bench. He started gesturing out to the mound, rubbing his hands down the side of his face to his heart and then extending his arms to the side of his body. "Control your emotions, Jethro," he was shouting, but Jethro wasn't paying any attention.

Kevin Youklis who had come into the game as a defensive substitute was due up next. As he headed to the plate, he was called back to the bench. "Batting for Kevin Youklis," Bob Sheppard announced, "in the sixth spot in the order will be," he paused as if looking at an unfamiliar name, "Zachary Shinbone."

Zachary Shinbone wearing the number 00 started walking toward the plate.

Joe Torre turned to Mel Stottlemyre. "Who the fuck is Zachary Shinbone?"

"I don't know," Mel replied, "but it looks like Jethro does."

On the mound, Jethro was fidgeting noticeably. Instead of pounding the ball into his mitt, he was walking around the rubber looking confused and uneasy.

"What's going on?" Joe Buck wondered killing time. Fox TV statisticians were furiously trying to figure out who Zach Shinbone was. They handed Buck a note. "It looks like they slipped him on the roster before tonight's game. With everything going on, no one noticed. He has never played pro ball before."

In the Yankee dugout, Joe Torre knew that he had a problem, a big one.

"Do you want me to go out and talk to him?" Stottlemyre asked.

"Not this time," Joe replied. "I don't think this is a pitching problem. Just in case, get Gordon ready in the bullpen, QUICK." He walked over to Dr. Phil. "Let's go," he said. With that, Joe Torre and Phil McGraw headed to the mound.

"In all my years of baseball, I have never seen this before," Tim McCarver screamed into the mike. Jethro is getting a visit on the mound from his therapist."

Terry Francona was out of the Red Sox dugout and running towards the home plate umpire. "They can't do that. Send him back."

The umpire was scrambling. This situation was not covered in the basic handbook. He called his fellow umps together for a conference.

"What great theatre," Joe Buck was shouting. "This game will go down as one of the greatest in baseball history."

On the mound, Joe and Phil were listening to Jethro moan. "You don't understand," Jethro said, "I can't pitch to him."

"We can't walk him," Joe said. "He is the winning run."

"Tell me what's troubling you, young man," Dr. Phil said, savoring the moment. This was therapist's heaven.

Jethro started talking, "Zach and I grew up together in Pea Patch. Everything we did, he was just a little bit better. When we ran track, he would beat me by a nose. In ping-pong, he would always win twenty-one to nineteen. If I wanted to date a girl, she liked him better. If there was one spot left on the all-star team, he would get it."

"This would be a perfect time to confront those demons," Dr. Phil offered, "on the big stage of life in front of the world."

But Jethro wouldn't calm down. "If I pitch to him, I'll get two strikes, and then he will hit one out of the park."

Joe had heard enough. He was ready to call for Gordon when he saw Mel Stottlemyre waiving frantically from the dugout, pointing towards the bullpen. Gordon was bending over holding his arm.

Meanwhile, the umps were walking out to the mound like the Four Horsemen of the Apocalypse.

Meanwhile, George Steinbrenner was pacing in the owners box.

Meanwhile, Jethro was starting to blubber.

Joe was almost ready to blubber, too. Suddenly, just as the umpires arrived, Hoss Bodine who had been approaching the mound unnoticed from the other direction grabbed the ball out of Jethro's hand. "Hoss Bodine moving from DH to pitcher," he told the umps.

Torre was about to say something but changed his mind. Dr. Phil put his arm around Joe's shoulder. "Let's go back to the dugout for a nice cry. You can talk, and I will listen."

"I'll say it again," Joe Buck screamed in the booth, "I've never seen anything like this."

"And you never will," McCarver added.

As everyone returned to their positions, Hoss started his warm-ups. His windup was unconventional. He circled his arm three times and wiggled his hips before he threw. "Is that Mo, Larry or Curly?" A-Rod asked Derek Jeter.

"It looks more like a Teenage Mutant Ninja Turtle," Jeter replied.

Hoss finished his warm-ups. Zachary Shinbone stepped into the box.

"Who would have thunk it?" Joe Buck cried. "Hoss Bodine facing down Zachary Shinbone for the American League pennant."

Chapter 27

Jorge Posada took a look into the Yankee dugout as if to say, "Do you really want to go through with this?" Hoss' pitches were slow, down the middle of the plate and not fooling anyone. Unfortunately, Joe Torre didn't have a choice. Baseball rules dictate that a new pitcher face at least one batter.

"Walk him, skip," Mel Stottlemyre suggested. "Randy Johnson is almost ready in the bullpen."

In their skybox, George Steinbrenner and Donald Trump were starting to posture. Neither could decide whether to be the triumphant victor or the disgusted loser. Like a stock analyst that had no idea which way the market was going, they both were starting to hedge their positions.

"The biggest payroll in the majors, and we can't strike out Zachary Shinbone," George lamented.

"If this was the Apprentice," Donald replied, "I would consider firing them all."

Hoss wound up and delivered the first pitch. Zach swung and hit a drive down the left field line.

"If it stays fair, it's gone," Joe Buck said. Fifty-five thousand fans held their breath. George Steinbrenner closed his eyes and clenched his fists. "Just foul," Buck announced as every New Yorker in every seat and every bar and every living room took a deep breath.

Hoss took a new ball from the ump and delivered again. Wham! Another drive, this time down the right field line.

"Oh my," screamed McCarver, "what a shot. It's a…foul ball, foul by inches two Ruthian drives in a row, both of them in the upper deck. It looks like this Shinbone fellow has got Hoss' number."

Joe Torre had seen enough. The phone from the bullpen rang. Randy Johnson was ready. Joe stood on the dugout steps, whistled to get Hoss' attention and held up four fingers, the universal sign in baseball instructing a pitcher to issue an intentional walk. Hoss looked at the signal. At first, he seemed confused. Then, he got a weird look on his face and started to smile. He walked to the back of the mound and started rubbing the ball furiously. He stepped back on the rubber. Jorge Posada stood up behind the plate with his arm extended to signal the intentional ball. Hoss peered in to the plate.

"He doesn't know what the sign means, Joe," Mel started screaming. "He doesn't know you want to walk him. He thinks you're calling for some special pitch."

"I can't do anything about it," Joe said. "We've been to the mound already. Hoss has to face at least one batter."

"We need to do something," Mel was frantic.

"You need to have some faith and pray."

"What the fuck," Joe said as he looked around. Al Sharpton had arrived in the dugout unannounced. He was standing next to Dr. Phil McGraw. "Have some faith, gentlemen," the Reverend repeated. "This is my domain."

For the first time in his life, Joe Torre was speechless. He turned to his pitching coach. After a couple of seconds, he said to Mel, "Let's sit down and watch the game."

Hoss wound up. At the top of his motion, his arm speed slowed and with a flip of his wrist, he delivered a 'Euphis' pitch toward the plate. High in the air, looking like a slow-pitch softball toss, it inched its way towards home. Zachary adjusted his stance at the plate, took a hitch and swung. He hit a drive towards straight away center, the deepest part of Yankee Stadium.

"He's hit a long drive," Joe Buck roared.

What happened next will go down in baseball lore forever with the likes of the Babe's called shot and Mickey Owens' dropped third strike. This is how John Sterling called it.

"What a drive! That ball is high. It is far. It's going to be way out of here. The Red Sox have a one-run lead. Wait. Wait a minute. It hit something. The ball hit something. It hit a bird. It's falling back to earth. It must have hit a seagull. The ball and the bird are both falling back to the field. Abner is under it, I mean under them in centerfield. He's caught one. The other fell to the ground. Did he catch the ball or the bird? Oh my! Where are Alphonse and Gaston when we need them? Did he catch the ball or the bird? The umpire is running out to center. Brian Roberts has already scored. Zach Shinbone is coming around third. The ump is looking in his mitt. He caught the...BALL!!! The umpire is signaling an out. Theeeeeeeeeeeeee Yankees winnnnnnnnnnnnnnnnnnn! The Yankees win the pennant. Take over, Susan. I need to catch my breath."

The capacity crowd erupted. George Steinbrenner gave Donald Trump a big hug. In the dugout, Al Sharpton yelled "Hallelujah" and pointed his hands to the sky. The Yankee players ran to the mound and jumped into the traditional dog pile. Phil McGraw, with a big smile on his face, started pointing to his temple, taking credit for the victory as if it was his calming presence that had been the winning factor. Only Joe Torre seemed subdued. He picked up his lineup card and very quietly started walking to the clubhouse. “I think I am getting too old for this game Mel,” was the only thing that he said. He did, however, give Al Sharpton a ‘good-job-kid pat on the butt’ on his way out.

Chapter 28

Thus, the 2005 Yankees won the American League pennant. Their World Series victory was far less dramatic. Without the diversions of the Pea Patch Festival, the boys were unstoppable. They beat the Cardinals four straight. Jethro and Abner each threw complete game shutouts. Randy Johnson and Mike Mussina won games three and four. Hoss, Abner and Jethro broke almost every offensive World Series record, hitting, slugging, runs scored and runs batted in. Ironically, no one really cared. The Yanks had beaten the Red Sox in the greatest series in history. The rest was anti-climatic.

After the season, Brian Cashman sat down with the boys to talk long-term contract, but they really weren't interested. Jethro said he missed his friends and his mama. He had come up north to help win the pennant, and that was now accomplished. Besides, compared to moonshining and stock car racing, he found baseball boring. All he wanted to talk about was that he finally got the best of Zachary Shinbone. Abner decided that instead of playing another season, he would rather hang out with his big brother Jethro. He bought a nice house with his World Series check and moved in with Lila and his drinking buddy from Central Park, Jackson. Hoss moved back to Daisy's house and spent most of his days sitting in his favorite chair and watching a video tape of game seven. Religiously, he watched Oprah and Dr. Phil every day.

Cletus resigned his job as special assistant to the general manager and resumed his former duties as clubhouse attendant. The interaction with the players was what he enjoyed the most.

Joe Torre and Mel Stottlemyre both retired. After the World Series Championship, there were no more worlds to conquer. They left at the top of their game with a solid place in Yankee history. Joe said that his heart couldn't take another season. He and Mel started a free baseball camp for the poor children of the city. Together, they worked for many years developing the Major Leaguers of the future.

George Steinbrenner sold the team. He was a smart enough businessman to know that with ratings at an all time high, he would never get a better price. Besides, the time to sell was not when you wanted out, but when someone wanted to buy. After the playoff ratings, every media company in the world wanted a piece of the world's greatest sports franchise. In his later years, the Boss devoted his time to his thoroughbreds. He went on to win three Kentucky Derby's. Whatever one could say about his methods, George had what it took to be a winner. For fun and to stay in the spotlight, he served on several city boards and commissions with his good friend, Al Sharpton, and he produced his own version of 'The Apprentice' called 'The Boss'.

Brian Cashman stayed on with the new owners. During the transition of ownership, he negotiated a piece of the team for himself becoming at the age of thirty-five, the youngest owner in baseball. An adrenalin junky, Brian stayed with the team for the rest of his career. To his last day, he always referred to the 'Pea Patch Season' as his favorite.

Not unexpectedly, Daisy's relationship with Al Sharpton ended abruptly after the season. She made a comfortable living as the boys' agent, booking their appearances and helping ghostwriters publish their biographies. She transformed her home into a museum. For many years, pilgrims traveled to Pea Patch to visit the shrine of the most recent Yankee legend. Every year in January, she entertained Brian Cashman on his annual trip to beg the boys to make a comeback. She also served on the President's Council for Literacy, promoting reading and education in rural areas of America.

The Reverend Al Sharpton remained a close friend to the family. He brought the boys to many of his political rallies and parlayed their fame to a victorious campaign for Mayor of New York. During two successful terms, the racial tensions in New York City abated, and the city prospered.

Immediately after the season, Dr. Phil published a book entitled, "Pea Patch, Profiles in Empowerment." A day-to-day journal of the 2005 season, the book portrayed his genius in taking three kids from the cornfields and turning them into Yankee legends. The message was clear to every Little League mom in America. Buy the book and your boy will become a Hall of Famer. The paperback edition was number one on the New York Times bestseller list for forty-two weeks.

That leaves us with two final pieces of business. What was the real story behind the nickname, Hoss, and where did the boys get their great athletic ability? In third grade, Eugene's class did a spring concert. All the boys and girls with good voices were given singing parts. The ones that couldn't sing were given costumes. Eugene was dressed up like a horse. In the first act, he came galloping onto the stage to announce the first songs. To keep him from getting his feelings hurt, his brothers told him that the costumes were given to the best actors, not the worst singers. Eugene was so proud that he wore his costume day and night for months until the fabric wore out. The nickname, Hoss, was born and stuck with him amongst much speculation of his other attributes for the rest of his life.

As for the boys' athletic ability, let's just say that someday there might be tests to analyze all the components of their special family moonshine, and that some of the ingredients might be found to be illegal substances innocently crafted by ancestors who knew nothing about baseball or the New York Yankees. That, however, will be the beginning of another story.

CPSIA information can be obtained at www.ICGtesting.com
Printed in the USA
LVOW100816231211

260742LV00002B/91/P